OHIO DOMINICAN U ⟨⟩ W9-BCR-756
LIBRARY
1216 SUNBURY ROAD
COLUMBUS, OHIO 43219-2099

OHIO
DOMINICAN
UNIVERSITY™

SINCE 1911

Donated by
Floyd Dickman

SHIP *of* FIRE

ALSO BY MICHAEL CADNUM

Cadnum
dnum, Michael.
ip of fire

OCT 2004
Received
Ohio Dominican

SHIP
of
FIRE

Michael Cadnum

VIKING

VIKING
Published by Penguin Group
Penguin Young Readers Group, 345 Hudson Street, New York, New York 10014, U.S.A.
Penguin Books Ltd, 80 Strand, London WC2R 0RL, England
Penguin Books Australia Ltd, 250 Camberwell Road, Camberwell, Victoria 3124, Australia
Penguin Books Canada Ltd, 10 Alcorn Avenue, Toronto, Ontario, Canada M4V 3B2
Penguin Books (N.Z.) Ltd, 182-190 Wairau Road, Auckland 10, New Zealand

First published in 2003 by Viking, a division of Penguin Young Readers Group

1 3 5 7 9 10 8 6 4 2

Copyright © Michael Cadnum, 2003
All rights reserved

LIBRARY OF CONGRESS CATALOGING-IN-PUBLICATION DATA
Cadnum, Michael.
Ship of fire / by Michael Cadnum.
p. cm.
Summary: In 1587, sailing to Spain on board Sir Francis Drake's ship
"Elizabeth Bonaventure," seventeen-year-old surgeon's apprentice Thomas
Spyre finds that, with the sudden death of his master, he must take over as
ship's surgeon and prove his skill not only as a doctor but also as a fighter
when he is enlisted by Drake to face battle.
ISBN 0-670-89907-0 (hardcover)
[1. Apprentices—Fiction. 2. Physicians—Fiction. 3. Seafaring life—Fiction.
4. Drake, Francis, Sir, 1540?-1596—Fiction.
5. Great Britain—History—Elizabeth, 1558-1603—Fiction.] I. Title.
PZ7.C11724Sh 2003 [Fic]—dc21 2003005832

Printed in U.S.A.
Set in Granjon
Book design by Nancy Brennan

Without limiting the rights under copyright reserved above, no part of this publica-
tion may be reproduced, stored in or introduced into a retrieval system, or transmit-
ted, in any form or by any means (electronic, mechanical, photocopying, recording
or otherwise), without the prior written permission of both the copyright owner and
the above publisher of this book. The scanning, uploading, and distribution of this
book via the Internet or via any other means without the permission of the publisher is illegal and punishable by law. Please purchase only authorized electronic edi-
tions, and do not participate in or encourage electronic piracy of copyrighted mate-
rials. Your support of the author's rights is appreciated.

For Sherina

Shadow fish
around the shadow
of your hand

SHIP *of* FIRE

Chapter

I

THE BEAR WAS LED INTO THE PIT, AND the dogs went mad, barking and lunging, straining their tethers.

"This will be the day of our great good fortune, Thomas," my master William Perrivale cried through the din. "Have you ever seen such a beast?"

I answered with a laugh. "Never, indeed, my lord!"

In truth, I was host to the gravest misgivings.

The bear was indeed a fierce brute, bound about his middle by a coarse hemp rope. The five dogs leaped, shrilling at the smell of him. For all their tumult, they were kept from setting eyes on their prospective opponent by a stained linen screen.

The great bruin sniffed the air, shuffling sideways to the extent of his heavy rope. This was a beast new to London, just arrived by ship from the far seas and deep forests, according to ale-house rumor. My master leaned forward over the partition of our stall and appraised the dark furred giant. He gave a satisfied nod at what he saw.

The Bear Garden was filling with its usual throng, merry noblemen and even merrier poor folk. Bright-eyed gamesmen accepted bets from every purse. A recent act of Parliament had forbade bear-baiting on the Lord's Day, and it was murmured that such sport might be closed down altogether—some preachers expressed the opinion that the sport encouraged vice. And so the traditional Thursday fight was all the more popular, and even our Queen Elizabeth was rumored to place a bet by proxy, one or two of the silked-and-plumed noblemen among us wagering royal gold.

"I bet my entire purse," cried my master, raising his voice to get the attention of one of the Bear Garden employees. "My entire fat purse I bet on the bear's victory."

"And how much, my lord, would your purse weigh?" said Bob Chute, the veteran gamesman not wanting to accept a wager not easily paid off.

My master had schooled in Magdalen College, Oxford, and had earned a name as one of the best medical men. He was now well established in London as a merciful and worthy doctor who lived by his knowledge of phlegm and spleen. He spent effort and silver on teaching me, reciting with me the wisest medical writings under Heaven, from Hippocrates to his own Latin discourses on medicinal roots.

Further, he swore that he would live up to his loyalty to my deceased father by making me, inch by inch, a gentleman. He hired a sword master from Mantua, the famous Giacomo di Angelo, to teach me the art of the rapier, and a scholar from Paris to teach me the history of kings and emperors of the world.

But my worshipful master William had a weakness—recurring and overpowering—for games of chance. This gambling fever gripped him now as he tossed the leather coin sack in his hand. Bob Chute's smile gleamed with professional avarice.

"I wager my entire purse of new silver," my master asserted in a tone of care-free certainty. "I bet that the bear will outlast the dogs, and more, that every dog will be flayed or gutted and flung to the penny-public." This was not the reckless wager it seemed. A sailor friend of my master had predicted the bear's fighting prowess at the Hart and Trumpet the night before.

Bob Chute cocked his head, ignoring the general hubbub. "To be doubled, coin for coin, if the bear dies," said the gamesman. "Or if the bearward judges the brute beyond recovery." Bearwards were wily men, and could coax a carcass back to life by blowing pepper into its nose.

"Done!" said my master with a laugh.

My heart sank. We could not afford such a heavy wager if we lost. The entire city of London, it seemed, took freshly painted wherries and other hire-craft across the river on such an afternoon, but our meager purses had forced us into a leaking, badly patched vessel, the boat fighting the strong current and nearly capsizing. One more unlucky afternoon, and we would have to pawn our cloaks—or worse, our swords.

Now the dog handlers soothed and kissed their fighters. Bear-dogs are even more fierce than ban-dogs, animals the law requires be tied or caged. The bear-fighting dog is bred and tutored to his craft, and this was a spirited pack, well muscled and trembling with eagerness.

The restless giant padded back and forth on the hard-packed earth, his rope alternately slack and taut as he paced. It was true that the bear did not look drunk on wine, as fighting cocks often were, or drugged with some sleeping philter, as a bear had been not a fortnight before. That creature had been so piebald and sluggish the crowd had howled the bearwards to shame, and a special display of minstrelsy had been added to calm us, players of string instruments and tambours, with merry dancing.

I had liked that music as well as any bear-fight, or even better. I often accompanied my master on his river-crossings to this district of the Rose Theater and taverns and cockpits, and even trugging shops—houses where whores plied their trade, arrayed in finest taffeta and silks. Bear-baiting is lusty sport, but before God I think I prefer a good story and a cup of strong cider.

Now, at a toss of the bearward's cap, the linen screen was whisked away, and the crowd roared as the five dogs gave full vent to their excitement. One particular dog, with livid scars along his flanks, I had seen in victorious battle before. This was the one creature who quietly lowered his body to the earthen floor, wasting little breath on making noise.

The chief bearward held up his hand, poised to signal the release of the fighters. An assistant hurried across the pit, and kicked away a walnut that had rolled from the cheapest seats. Yet another bearward smoothed out the dirt and sawdust, wet from a dogfight that had entertained the crowd before our arrival. The crowd was already hoarse with shouting, but at this delay the outcry was beyond belief, roars and laughter, curses, drunk and sober men alike crying, "Get on with it!"

Still the bearwards delayed, outfitted in one blue stocking and one red like many minstrels and dancers. Perhaps they relished their momentary power over man and beast, and one of them took pains to produce a rake and smooth out some nearly imaginary rough spot in the pit.

I cupped my hands around my mouth and added my voice to the deafening clamor.

The chief bearward's hand swept down in a courtly bow.

In an instant the pack was loose.

Chapter

2

•

BLOOD FLEW.

William cupped his hand over his eyes, as so often before, and beseeched me, "Thomas, tell me when the bear stands alone."

I myself preferred to play at bowls, and had won a wager on a bright day or two, when some gamesman had not watered the grass so heavily an honest young man could not pitch a ball true. Bear brawls favored the dogs, which, though small in stature, attacked in gangs. Once attached by their teeth a pack of dogs could bleed a bear, if it took an hour. But it was no sure outcome, either way, and many a day at the Bear Garden concluded with a cart of dead dogs creaking down to the river bank.

Scar-flank, the most seasoned dog, attacked quietly, straight for the bear's hind legs. He locked his jaws deep in the fur, and worried and worked, fighting deep and deeper into the sinews and vessels of the bear's limb. Blood started, the scarred dog's muzzle going dark, his forepaws sodden, an increasing flow of scarlet.

The great bear roared and showed his teeth. Four dogs had him by the haunch and forelimbs, a dog to each extremity, each with an iron fang-hold, hanging on. A fifth fighter, a young, yellow bounder, took the bear's roars as a challenge, and seized the bear's snout with his teeth. The bruin lunged one way and another, shaking his huge head sideways, and up and down, but the dog sank his fangs deeper into the bear's upper snout while his legs flailed round and about like boneless rags.

The great carnivore charged ahead, and at once reached the extremity of the hemp cord. The shock was so severe the rope stump, an ancient piling sunk into the earth, shivered as though it would pull right out of its place. Dust rose. The bear rolled suddenly, and in his tumble, trapped two dogs under his bulk. The two dogs screamed, unable to climb to their feet, and as the bear rose to his haunches he seized a white-and-yellow dog in an encircling embrace.

This hug was so fierce, and so long in duration, that the dog's eyes rolled and his tongue hung from the side of his mouth. With a snap, the pit-dog's backbone broke. His hind legs dangled and the crowd let out a shout as the mortally injured fighter was flung away.

Surely, I thought, we are in luck after all.

The congregated vagrants, merchants, and gentlemen all clamored and exchanged late wagers. It was here, among the gentlemen's stalls, that trugs—wandering prostitutes—often found clients. Here was where whore-masters set the price and gave directions to the pick-hatch—the house of venery and sin—down one alley or another beyond the theaters. But no one had eyes now for anything but the torn ground of the bear pit.

I suspected it was a sin to seek Christ Jesus' help in winning a wager.

But even so, I prayed.

The growling of the dogs had ceased, four torn bodies in the pit. It was difficult to credit that moments before these animals had been fighters.

And yet, stubbornly, locked onto the bear's hind leg, Scar-flank was still very much alive, dragging along behind as the bear struggled to turn around. When no other dog remained alive, the scarred brawler stayed right there, jaws locked around the limb.

"Tell me, William," said my master, shielding his eyes with his hand. "What news?" No dog at all made a sound now, and even the crowd was more quiet. The heavy, phlegmy cough of the bear was loud.

The bruin was in mortal trouble, his blood saturating the pit. But how could I put this cruel tidings into words?

"You have eyes in your head, Thomas Spyre," my master insisted. "How goes the battle?"

Scar-flank clung hard.

Chapter

3

●

THE EVENING HAD TURNED SHOWERY, SPITS of rain falling from a mottled sky.

We knew it was useless to talk. We were relieved to leave the bear pit and the yelling crowd behind. Maybe, I hoped, this would see the last of William's wagering for a good long while.

My master stepped around stews of human waste in the crooked lanes. Householders were required by law to burn rubbish every few weeks, and the stink of kitchen leavings put to fire, mutton bones, cheese butts, and rank apple cores, did nothing to sweeten the air. The spattering rain dampened the smoldering heaps and made the stink worse.

"Only one little dog," said my master, in a tone of dismal wonder. "Only one, flea-blistered, unconquerable little pit-scamp." He sighed and shook his head. "I would not have believed it possible."

When a dimpled lass stepped before us and lifted her ample skirts my master stopped in his tracks. She was plump and desirable enough, and she held her petticoats up high so we could see the top of her stockings and her bare and very pretty knees.

"A good evening to you, my lords," said the young woman.

My master gave a polite bow, and returned her greetings with a world-weary air. Even now, though, some of his habitual good cheer was returning. "Madam," he said, "you see before you two paupers. We are not worth your trouble."

She hiked her skirts even higher, offering a view of pink thighs. "Surely," she returned, "my lords have enough coin for a sporting tumble."

There was the softest whisper behind us—a footstep.

At once William put his hand to his sword. "Quick, Thomas, look around you."

A wiry male figure darted back from behind me as I spun. I seized him by the padded shoulder of his jerkin, and flung him hard against the tavern wall. The young woman, with a flurry of skirt and lingering scent of rose water, hurried off down the street.

It was a common ploy—distracting a man with a whore's show of leg while the cutpurse darted in, did his work, and ran off.

Now the nip—as street thieves are called—let out a whistle even as I trapped him against the wall. Two hulking assistants, older men armed with truncheons, strode from a smoke-choked alley. They showed their teeth in confident yellow smiles, their loose stockings thrust into muddy shoes.

"Gentlemen footpads," said my master, addressing these two newcomers, "spare yourselves the sweat. See here, my purse is as thin as the Pope's mercy. I have just lost a mighty wager, and Thomas here has a rapier made in Milan."

I had released the nip and drawn my blade, a shining length of steel. A few Englishmen still sported broadswords, believing the increasingly popular French and Italian weapons to be unmanly, too quick and subtle. Nevertheless, I liked the feel of my rapier, and had practiced until I could make the blade sing.

I cut a figure with my blade now, the point humming, and both hairy-fisted men stopped where they were, their full attention on the gleaming tip. One of them made a motion with his club, warding off my blade clumsily, and I put the point of my sword up to his chin, parting his beard. I held it steady, my arm and wrist strong from hours of swordplay with my teacher.

The truth was I had never so much as pricked a living man. I always practiced sword-work in the customary over-warm pads and mask. Like many other seventeen-year-olds in London, I could play a fighter but knew little about actual killing. Nevertheless, the two tall men took me for a practiced bladesman.

One truncheon fell onto the wet street, and the other was waved weakly, as though in apology.

The lean little nip, the master of the small gang, was crying out merrily, "I know this fine lord!"

"Yes, and I know you." My master put a hand to his graying beard, his gaze inward in the act of recall. "It's little Bruce Hollings!" he said at last with a laugh.

"Yes, my lord, whose fever you broke with a cup of mustard water," said the street thief, looking up at my master with admiration and gratitude. "I didn't recognize you after these seven years. You're the best physician in London, with a young gentleman scholar apprentice now, I see."

"Thomas is the son of a departed friend of mine, a man who penned Greek as you or I would draw breath."

"Sir, I am honored," said Bruce Hollings, giving me a fair bow, one leg forward, his rain-dappled hat removed with a flourish from his head.

I gave a half bow of my own, much relieved that on this night I would not see my blade draw blood. I gave a nod to the two roughs, and, with a smooth flourish I had practiced under my sword-tutor's eye, sheathed my sword.

"I thought you were in the stocks as a whipjack, Bruce," said my master, hunting through his mantle for a coin. He gave me a hopeful nod, but indeed I had only an old penny, one of debased silver from early in our glorious Queen Elizabeth's reign, before she had improved the coinage.

Although my master was of lofty birth, with a small estate in Devon, his family was as poor as they were long-established. He had many patients, both wealthy and impoverished, attending them in his chambers on Leadenhall Street, just inside the city wall. My master believed as the Scriptures teach us, that if we show charity to the least of folk we show it to Our Lord.

"For only a year or so I worked the whipjack's trade," said Bruce confidingly.

A whipjack is a beggar with a forged license to seek alms. Licensed beggars are usually old mariners, spent by years of service with the Queen's sailing fleet, jaundiced or scurvy-spent, if not reduced to amputated stumps or blind from cannon sparks. My master had a soft heart for sailors, having signed as ship's surgeon on a vessel bound for the Canaries as a young man, a voyage he now recalled as rich with every manner of adventure. When he drank enough beer he would even tell the tale of how he had once seen a mermaid.

"I had to give up whipjacking," Bruce was recalling. "It took patience and a sort of acting talent you might see at the Rose Theater, or the Globe, but fell beyond me."

I pressed the old penny into the nip's palm and he offered a wry smile of thanks in return. "Your master once cured the Lord of the Admiralty himself of a deadly ague," said Bruce Hollings. "Everyone on both banks of the river knows that a greater and kinder master of physic never lived."

"He is as you say," I agreed.

I never wearied of hearing my master praised, but I was concerned in this slowly increasing rain. An apprentice depends on his master for coin, and now that my purse was entirely empty we were two of the poorest men in England. We would have to go into debt simply to take a boat back home across the roaring current of the Thames.

"I lost the contents of my purse just now," my master was saying, "trusting the fighting skill of that storied Russian bear."

"Alas, good my lord!" said Bruce. "Not that bear everyone was talking about, for the last week?"

"That very animal," said my master.

"That Muscovite brute of a bear," said Bruce, "was starved weak in a cage out behind St. Savior's church."

"Starved?" my master echoed bleakly.

"I wouldn't have bet a thimble of vinegar on the poor beast," said Bruce. He showed perhaps more than a glimmer of pleasure in being, in this instance, wiser than a well-known master of medicine.

"Forgive me, Thomas," said my master giving me a sidelong glance.

"We can't take coin," said Bruce, "from two such unlucky gentlemen on a damp evening. Peter and Jamie here will see you across the river."

Peter, or perhaps Jamie, flipped the penny back to me, and I was grateful to see it return. It was all the money we had under Heaven, and would have to last us until a sea master staggered into our chambers with scurvy, or brought in one of his sailors half dead with yellow jack.

My master and I perched in a wherry, a river vessel, rowed by Peter and commanded by Jamie, who had teeth like a horse and a strong voice, calling the traditional river man's *way, make way,* the sing-song cry I had heard often as I drifted to sleep in my bunk.

Twilight lingered. The river was a void slashed with light, tallow-torches along either bank, and lanterns on the looming bridge not far from us downriver, casting streaking reflections on the brown water. The river was crowded with boats, each craft guided by an expert rower and kept well upriver from the troubled water around the London Bridge.

It was clear from the start that we should have come to some agreement with a more proficient wherry-keeper.

Peter and Jamie were friendly enough, now, but knew nothing about the river. Peter rowed all out of rhythm, one oar in the current while the other circled in the air.

"You'll see us drowned!" called Jamie from inside his hood.

Our wherry was drifting quickly downriver toward the arches and high, dark stalls of the bridge. The Thames, high with spring rain, was rumbling through the arches of the ancient structure. The white water seethed and tumbled, our boat turning one way and another in the boiling current.

"You told me you were a rowing man!" Jamie was exclaiming.

Peter was too overworked to retort, his yellow teeth exposed in a grimace of effort.

"Take the oars, Tom," said my master sharply.

Boats during spring floods often circled in a sudden whirlpool and collided with each other, and river men were famous for the vehemence of their curses. It was evident that Peter was far less skilled, or perhaps more drunk, than he had seemed. And the river, which had been rough enough on our way across earlier in the day, had grown more surly.

I stood in the unsteady craft, and at once nearly fell into the water.

Chapter

4

BUT I KNEW THE NATURE OF RIVERS.

I had been born in a village in the heart of Dartmoor, among sheep pens and shepherds' songs. When I was a small boy my father had taken me on day-long rambles out to the River Tavy. He had taught me how to pilot a rowboat. Now I steadied our wherry, using the oar as a lever against the mossy groin of the bridge.

I nearly toppled into the Thames as our craft slipped under the bridge, and into the gentle eddies that circulated in the river beyond.

"Well done, Tom," said my master, putting his hand on my shoulder.

Before my father followed my mother into Heavenly bliss, he penned a letter to the old friend he had known at the long oak tables of the university. As a ten-year-old boy with no more knowledge of the world than a field mouse, I had been carried by a friendly carter as far as the ruined abbey, where the Crown and Vixen shelters guests for a fee.

There I met a stranger down from London, wearing a physician's mantle and a city man's sword. I knew him at once from my father's promise, *You'll know he's a good man from the first.*

Now the rain had stopped, and the evening was warm.

Thankful to be alive, for a few moments of quiet we enjoyed the rising darkness on the river. The current was calmer here, the city a haphazard collection of candlelit windows and half-closed shutters, a scattering of cheerful lamps and embers as the smiths and brewers banked their fires, and through wide-flung shutters we could see wealthy folk lighting tapers to see their way up stairwells, their quaking shadows preceding them. The bank was marbled where slaughterhouses poured fat and blood down their gutters, and the heavy current foamed yellow where a brewery gushed dregs.

Ahead of us a great vessel was afloat in the river.

"Row down to the ship," my master urged, and Peter, so recently frightened, was a reformed boatman now, making timid but effective strokes with both oars. We coursed out to mid-river, and made our way down to the tall ship.

It was unusual to see a fighting ship so far upstream from the boating yards. With four masts and two castles—elevated wooden structures for guns and archers fore and aft—the vessel towered over our river-vessel. The ship's name in gilt letters was hard to make out in the growing dark, but my master knew ships and their masters, having loved them all his life.

"It's the *Golden Lion,*" my master breathed. "Anchored upriver, closer to the finer houses, so gentlefolk can board her." Lords and ladies supported Queen Elizabeth's hungry efforts to rebuild her forces with occasional, much-needed patronage. Sometimes a man of noble name purchased a berth for an adventurous son—or for himself.

Peter and Jamie were both open-mouthed at the sight of the great cable that angled up from the river, and the helmeted head that looked down over the side of the ship, a soldier, judging from his mail shirt and his gloves. Laughter drifted down from the ship, ladies, no doubt being shown the cannon and the swivel-guns, excited by the sight of so much power afloat. And I was open-mouthed, too.

I had never come so close to a warship.

"God keep you, sergeant," called my master, who always knew the proper tone of voice and title in addressing a stranger.

"And you, my lord," said the soldier, gazing down at us. He wore a flowing red mustache, and held a boarding pike, a tall, gleaming weapon, polished so it reflected torch light. London had been alive with rumors. There was trouble on the wide seas. King Philip of Spain had ordered the detaining and harassment of English merchants in his ports, and tavern whispers told of an even more sinister turn of events.

In this year of Our Lord 1587, Spanish ships cowed the known world. They parted every sea, freighting gold from the New World, sometimes harried by a brave English privateer. The proud Spanish had grown impatient with this nuisance. Tavern reports held that the king of Spain was building an Armada, a navy bigger than any ever seen before.

Fear of this war-fleet woke us long before dawn, dread shadowing our steps. Spain was the richest, and best armed, kingdom in the world. Our smaller ships and more meager navy would be as chaff against this storm.

Brew-house rumor further held that the famous sea captain Sir Francis Drake was storing shot and gunpowder, gathering a force in the southern port of Plymouth, preparing a fighting voyage to destroy the Spanish warships before they could sail north.

"Surely the Spanish," said my master with an air of hopeful bravado, "have no idea what an English sword can do."

"Spain's a dog needs whipping," said the soldier. He shifted his pike and gave a quiet laugh. "And a pricking, too."

As pleasing as these strong words sounded, they did little to dispel my unease at the thought of our small kingdom locked against Spanish might.

We sat there in the current-rocked wherry as gentlefolk were handed down into river craft and departed the *Golden Lion*.

And then, as the darkness became complete and the ship was little more than a vague, darker shape in the night, we saw the bright splashes as her sweeps, the long oars ships use in the absence of wind, turned her bow downriver, and the current took her.

I had long dreamed of sailing with a famous ship's master and winning glory under sail. It was a boyish longing, I knew, and beneath the dignity of a young man destined to practice medicine.

Nevertheless my pulse quickened at the sight.

Chapter

5

MY MASTER LIT THE STUB OF A CANDLE downstairs, where the fragrance of roasting cheese and toasted bread made my stomach growl.

In debt for a month's rent, we had tried to avoid the eye of the tavern's owner, and we succeeded, tiptoeing up the stairs. My master was the perfect example of how a man of name should look, from his quilted doublet, with its high shoulders and tapered profile, down to the fine red riding hose on his legs. I, for my own part, looked much the young gentleman, if I may say so. My hair is copper-red, and damp weather has always caused it to become tangled and knotted, but I am tall enough to look down on many men. To further improve my appearance, my master sent me to a skilled tailor, in those seemingly long-past days when we could afford one.

William and I sat to our supper, a pilchard so old it curled up at either end, the ancient fish giving off a sharp smell. We ate that, and a heel of barley loaf patched with mold, cut evenly down the middle with a knife.

"So that's it," said my master when we had supped, with a degree of ceremony so we would not feel as poor as we were.

My master had put on a velvet robe, and sported the cap he wore indoors, the one embroidered with golden thread. To see him you'd have thought him as rich as the owner of a counting-house, where foreign coin was weighed and exchanged for the Queen's silver.

"That's it, and here we are," he said with an air of affable finality. "Hungry and thirsty and surrounded by dark." He uttered this stark knowledge as though to make light of our condition, and nearly succeeded.

"Many men must have lost good coin," I ventured, "betting on a cozened bear." To *cozen* was to cheat, or to make a false appearance. Cozened wine was a mix of dye and water, and cozened beef was bulked out with red sawdust.

My master gave me a sad smile, the shadows of the sputtering candle dancing in the folds of his robe. "You'll make a wise physician someday, Tom," he said. "To calm the sufferer is often to heal him."

I had much to learn about medicine, but as always I was grateful for my master's kind encouragement.

"I want to ask you to forgive your foolish master, Tom," he said. "If it please you. I shall find the inner resolve—I promise—to cease from wagering."

He had said this before on such occasions.

I could remember my mother mostly as a smile and a warm touch, a kiss on my forehead. I did possess one clear memory—vivid and plain as though I were still there in my parents' cottage. One Lady Day she gave me a fragment of honeycomb on a wooden plate, and cautioned me not to eat "the poor, spent bodies of the bees, only the wax and sweetness."

She died before I had seen four Easters, and in truth I wonder if this deep-dyed memory was a real morning from my life, stored in my soul, or the result of my spirit's handiwork, creating a recollection when there was none. But I do remember her reading from Foxe's well-known book of Protestant martyrs, and believe I hear her voice even now, sometimes, reciting prayers.

I owed my master my learning, and, thanks to his roof and bread, my life. And yet I did wish I could find a way to tell my master that it was time he lived up to his promise to give up wagering. Could he not make the most solemn oath, his right hand on Holy Scripture, the sort no one would break?

"My lord," I began, "I do believe we must change the way we live."

"And we shall!" he asserted, slapping the table.

"But in months past we had a choice, my lord," I continued. "Now, left with only one bad penny, and forced to hide from our landlord—"

I let my thought complete itself in his mind.

"I shall become a new man," he said in a tone of finality, even resolve.

"My lord, you must," I said.

He was not pleased at such honesty from me, for a moment. But his eyes softened at once, and he nodded, gazing into our cold hearth. "Thomas, I will."

There was a tapping at the door. It was a knock we

recognized, and then there followed a continuing, more persistent pounding, which we recognized all the more.

"We are caught," said my master, with at least a little humor.

Our rooms were over a tavern where aldermen gathered to talk about the sprawl of new, poorly joined buildings on Shoreditch, and the way the farmland of Finsbury Fields was being lost, covered over with the high-peaked houses of rich tanners and ship owners. Scholars took beer in the tavern, too, mathematicians from the lecture halls of Leadenhall, men who could predict the eclipse of a moon centuries from now, or recount one that had darkened Earth many ages in the past.

Ship's carpenters drank their ale here, as well, along with those who called themselves gentlemen. The Lord Mayor himself once took a slice of cheese in the Hart and Trumpet. No one would call it a shame to live above a place where a gentle poet, Sir Philip Sidney, once wrote a sonnet in exchange for a tankard of the house's best wine, the same poet whom my master bled one day, opening a vein in his arm to ease a headache.

"Maybe we're mistaken," said my master in a whisper. "Perhaps some cook has cut off his finger." A pie maker had suffered just such an injury the year before, cleaving his left forefinger neatly from his hand. My master had looked on as I bound the wound, to the pie man's grateful satisfaction.

I hurried to the door, trying to believe that a patient must surely be downstairs, and, since the evening was well advanced, half expecting a knife wound or broken jaw, or some other drinking man's injury. This would put silver in our purse, and we could finish our supper with a bubbling pudding or—one of my favorites—fresh-baked bread smeared with rare marmalade.

To my distress, in stepped the man we both feared—the tavern owner and landlord of our chambers, Nicholas Nashe.

"Have no fear, good Nicholas," said my master lightly. "I'll have your rent by tomorrow's ebb tide, or I'm an ape."

I kept my mouth well shut, but wondered at my master's bold assertion. He was rightly considered a man of honor, but we had so little food in our cupboard that the mice had abandoned it and taken to nibbling his anatomy books on the shelf.

"There's a gentleman downstairs, my lord," said Nicholas, in a confidential whisper. "Dressed in a surgeon's mantle like your own, wearing a rapier with a rich agate-stone hilt, upon my faith."

"Is he ill, good Nicholas, or merely drunk?" my master asked in a tone of gentle exasperation. But it was a tone of relief, too—Nicholas was not demanding money.

Our landlord placed his hands together prayerfully. "He is known as a sometime ship's surgeon."

"Is he bleeding, or cold-sweating, or—"

"My lord, he is called Titus Cox, and he has swooned."

"Heaven protect us, I know the man!" My master was out of his chair. "But good Nicholas, he will not be the first gentleman to fall on the floor of the Hart and Trumpet and need assistance, surely."

"The last words he spoke, my lord," said Nicholas, "were 'show me to Doctor Perrivale.'" Nicholas delivered this imitation of another's voice, and a sick man at that, with theatrical skill, sounding in accent and tenor very much the mortally stricken gentleman.

My master strode toward the door, but Nicholas tugged at his sleeve, holding him back.

"He said more, my lord, words that made little sense to my ears," said Nicholas in a hoarse whisper. "In an effort to understand what the pitiable gentleman was trying to communicate," he added, "I took the liberty, my lord, of slipping this from his sleeve."

It was a scroll of vellum, the finest sheepskin, sealed with a crisp scarlet crown of wax, and tied around with a blue ribbon. The sight of the seal stopped my breath. I had seen such bright sealing wax, and pretty ribbon, carried by leather-jerkined men in the street, hurrying on some state business. Court documents bore such seals, commissions to have noble criminals arrested.

Death warrants, handed up to hangmen on the gallows, were marked with such wax, too.

My master hesitated to touch the scroll. London was a tangle of spies and government agents. It was reckless to learn another man's secrets.

He set the document aside, unread, but only after he had studied the seal and peered cautiously into the shadowy shaft of this important document.

Chapter
6

•

WE HURRIED DOWN THE STAIRS.

"Titus Cox is a good master of medicine, although he was never a man to cut a vein," my master was saying, trying to force a breezy confidence into his words. "He always preferred the leech."

Nearly any illness responded well to a copious bleeding, measured by the cupful. Most medical masters preferred to sever a vein with a lancet, a sharp blade made for that purpose, but there were those who praised the river leech. My master had trained me in both methods, to answer the needs of every variety of patient.

People needing a tooth pulled or an abscess pricked could see a barber. Such barbers were adept at binding wounds and draining pus, but most men and women with weight in their purses would prefer the attention of a surgeon. Surgeons rarely cut or even set a splint, relying on books and star charts to advise their patients. My master, however, set his hand to every aspect of the medical profession, and studied every drug, including the newly imported *tobecka,* which some doctors considered a cure-all.

I followed, but at the last moment I paused to work a wrinkle out of my stockings. They had been darned at the knee by my own needle. I worked the stitching around so it didn't show from the front. There was no way of knowing what knight or poet might be drinking here tonight.

The tavern was a cockpit of bright plumage. Every man dressed in tight-fitting stockings and a codpiece, to pad out his God-given manliness. Most of the men in the Hart and Trumpet that night had set aside a plumed cap, either soft and loose, in a manner considered French, or stiff and peaked, in a more English style. Even when a man of the town did not wear such a cap, he kept it nearby, as proof of his good taste.

But the place was subdued just now, a mere pale imitation of its usual liveliness, despite Mrs. Nashe's cheer and expert flattery—she was a woman who could nudge a Puritan into a smile.

I caught a glimpse of Jane, Nicholas's dark-haired daughter. She had brought me fresh-baked ale-cakes in recent weeks, and we'd shared a kiss or two when her mother was busy coaxing playwrights and drapers into paying off their accounts. Jane's eyes asked a question I could not answer.

A few gentlemen nodded greetings to my master, and extended the courtesy to me. I nodded in return, but kept what I trusted was a medical-man's solemnity in my bearing. Heads inclined in our direction as we knelt to attend our patient.

The man stretched out in the light from the hearth wore a velvet-lined mantle, and a city man's rich sword. His limbs were rigid and his eyes darting about, an unholy smile twitching his lips. Watery saliva streamed down his cheek. As he tried to extend his hand to greet my master, the arm jerked, and his feet spasmed, making awkward, uncontrolled running motions in the flickering firelight.

"My lord, is it the falling sickness?" asked Nicholas.

The symptoms did resemble *epilepsia*—epilepsy. But something about the way the stricken gentleman tried to rise, working hard to sit up, made me murmur a prayer. I had seen examples of epilepsy, attending a cobbler in Eastcheap who fell to the plank floor of his shop from time to time. The seizures were sometimes troubling to see, but they passed with no harm.

Titus tried to speak, but made only a choking sound. His eyes were full of feeling, fear, and recognition. Silently, I asked Heaven to spare my master's old friend.

"It's been a score of years, Titus," said my master gently, "since we drank wine together."

The stricken surgeon struggled to shape a word.

"Is it a stroke of God's hand?" the tavern owner was suggesting, the common phrase for a paralyzing fit. But the rigidity and trembling of the surgeon's arms and legs recalled only one evil illness to my mind.

"Or could it—" the tavern owner was saying, bending close to my ear. "Could it be poison?"

Chapter

7

NICHOLAS'S LAST GUESS WAS FAR FROM foolish.

There was much whispering about secret harm—poison, and the bodkin, a long, slender blade, easy to hide up a sleeve, the favorite weapon of both foreign and royal spies. People said that a Portuguese merchant had washed up well gnawed by fish, just downriver from Greenwich, the victim of both poison and stabbing with a slender knife. Portugal had recently been occupied by Spanish men-at-arms, and these days every Portuguese wine-seller was now suspect as a possible spy for King Philip of Spain.

A tailor fitting my new jerkin a few months before, when we had silver pennies to rub together, had murmured to me that a man heard murmuring in Spanish—or was it Portuguese?—on Fleet Street had been hustled into an ox-cart by heavily armed men. No one had seen him since.

"A Spanish spy could look as tall and well favored as you, young sir," said Ned the tailor, removing his spectacles and giving my face a measuring look. "If I may say so. And be evil through to his very soul."

Now my master had Nicholas send a tavern-boy to the Admiralty, with the message that one of the Queen's men was stricken. "Be quick!" my master added. The boy vanished into the dark street.

Nicholas had been pleased that a gentleman physician, tenant of the tavern, could attend to the crisis so quickly. But now he began to urge, in a hushed voice, that we hurry the sick man upstairs. "With speed, if it please you. Men do not drink and sup with a sick man lying before them."

That was true enough. Gentlemen, with brightly colored stockings and plumed caps, were entering the tavern, laughing as they stepped inside, only to be silenced by the sight of Titus stretched before them.

"What is your diagnosis, Thomas?" asked my master as we carried our patient up the stairs.

"Adder's venom?" I suggested. It was true that the snake's poison could be milked and kept in a vial. Our landlord remained downstairs, where we could hear his voice through the floorboards, lifted in a convincing show of good cheer.

My master stretched a blanket over the shivering surgeon in our chamber. "Such venom is a possibility, in truth," said William. "Although it's unlikely."

My master knew well what was wrong with our sufferer, and so did I, but he was testing my judgment.

I bent over our patient. His tongue and gums showed no lesions, but I knew the disease had passed far beyond that stage. Any examination of the gentleman's male member, and every other body part, would show no pustule, dry or wet—the malady was by many years too far advanced for that.

I said, "I fear this is no such easy complaint as poison."

We stepped to the sideboard, where, in richer days, a pitcher of wine always used to be kept. I said, in a low voice, "My lord, he is a very sick man."

"Do I need to pay an astrologer for his future, Thomas?" asked my master, with a bite to his voice.

"My lord, your fellow doctor suffers from the pox."

The subject of the pox was a painful one for both my master and myself.

That winter, a few days after Twelfth Night, with my master attending a noble woman in Windsor, I had removed a splinter from a shipwright's eye. As a medical man I was green, having nothing of my master's experience. But the shipwright, a West Country man like myself, begged me to pluck the wood from his eye, and I took up the challenge.

It was the first time I had ever used tweezers for such a delicate operation. The offending object was a stubborn little prick of spruce, and painful.

I had been so relieved to have the operation done—the shipwright's thanks still ringing in my ears, his silver in the purse at my belt—that I took a wherry across the river. I wanted to taste some of the south bank's stronger beer, and wanted to dance to some of the minstrels.

To my own surprise, I turned a corner, entered a door,

and stumbled right into a stew—a brothel. Once in, I kept on, into the entryway, led in by a mix of curiosity and ignorance. And perhaps a dash of lust.

Finding myself eye-to-eye with the white-bearded man in the short entry hall, I heard his phlegmy laugh, and his greeting: "Go on, young sir, and have a cup of beer with honest women."

It was a simple room, with a broad plank table, a large fireplace, and sweet-smelling rushes scattered on the floor, new hay and field flowers among them. With the smoke of seasoned wood and the perfume of hops in the air, it smelled like any clean inn along the road. Four women sat at the table, looking like prim servants, waiting for the master of the house to inspect them and pay their weekly allowance— but their clothes were undone about their tops. Even though I struggled not to gape and stare, I could not help myself.

When I heard a familiar voice demanding, *Let me past, whore-monger,* I turned to see my master, red-faced and ordering me to leave the place at once. I have never felt such gratitude and such shame at once.

"And will Titus recover?" my master asked now.

"If indeed he has the pox—and I have no doubt he does—" I could not complete my painful diagnosis, respectful of my master's feelings.

"Will he live?" William insisted in a tone of sad exasperation.

"No, my lord," I was forced to say. "God forgive us all, he will be as we see him now, but grow worse, over hours or perhaps days. He will surely die."

"So it is always with the pox, Thomas," said my master.

He was quiet for a moment, unable to continue out of sorrow for his old friend. "And Titus was a good Christian scholar, and knew Ovid by heart, and Sallust by the verse as well as any man. Ten or twenty years ago he galloped with a whore, or even some honest poxy woman—and he caught this curse."

It was called the *French welcome,* and I knew by my training that it killed as many, over time, as the plague. "My lord," I said now, my voice hoarse with feeling, "I neither touched nor spoke to any of the women in the trugging shop." This was not the first time I had made such a protest since my embarrassing rescue.

"If I hadn't passed by, in a hurry to try my luck," said William, "you'd confront the same ultimate illness as my poor friend. It must have been God's grace that let me see a familiar red-haired young man, big as any farmer, walking into the Wildrose Inn."

I nodded in red-faced agreement.

I was grateful for my escape from this evil. And yet, I wondered, why was such a dangerous sin so quick to stir desire? Shouldn't a merciful Heaven have created women less beautiful, more unlikely to warm the blood? Because certainly when I closed my eyes at night I still saw the women around the broad, unpainted plank table.

Besides, a certain spirit stirred in me. I wanted to hear my master explain a certain mystery—how a man could be wise on the question of pox, and on many other matters of man and God, and still lose his wealth down to the last bad penny betting on a bear notorious for its feebleness.

I was ready, with the question on my lips.

But loud steps crashed up the stairwell before I could speak. Nicholas, our landlord, burst into our room without the courtesy of a knock, wide-eyed.

"Soldiers!" he said breathlessly. "By Jesus, armed men are coming, good doctors, wearing helmets and carrying pikes." He let us consider this news, and added, "The tavern-boy has come back terrified, saying they are marching from the Tower itself—on their way here."

While not strictly yet a doctor, I was sometimes addressed as one, as an additional courtesy, and the title did not displease me.

But I was startled by this news, and so was my master, judging by his shocked silence.

Nicholas knotted his hands together, breathless with anxiety. "Could your patient be a *spy?*" He said the word with special emphasis, dropping his voice to a whip-lash whisper.

Chapter
8

•

"THIS SICK GENTLEMAN IS A DOCTOR," said my master in response. "He is in need of our medicine and your prayers. As you are in need of a cup of strong wine to strengthen your nerves."

"Oh, let me have my boys carry your sick gentleman friend out the back way, my lord," said Nicholas, "down into the alley, if it please you. He could prove to be an officer attempting to run off, a naval secret in his heart, before poison lay him down stiff—in my tavern!"

The sound of marching boots echoed down in the street, approaching closer, stride by stride. My master stretched himself to his full height, his mouth set in a determined line—but he had gone pale.

"I will not abandon my patient to the rats behind your kitchen," responded my master. "Bring us some wine, too."

"You could be arrested," said Nicholas, steadying his breath with effort. "For failing to resurrect him, or for preventing him from dying, both. Or either. Forgive me, but the Hart and Trumpet is mentioned at Court as a place where a scholar can order Canary wine in Latin, and be understood."

Nicholas was a fretful soul, but in his way he was no fool. Everyone knew that there was only one rack left in all of England. Torture was rarely used to force confession from outlaws in our Queen's frequently merciful reign. That one rack, made for stretching joint from joint, causing pain beyond imagining, was kept in the Tower, just a few minutes' march away.

We could not be put into chains simply for treating a man in disfavor with the Star Chamber, that deliberative body at the heart of our Queen's government. The cheerful beer-banter and laughter in the tavern downstairs fell silent, and the sound of heavy feet resounded from below.

"Nicholas," said my master, "you are the most white-livered man I have ever known."

Our landlord straightened his back and set his mouth. "I, my lord, am not the one with a document of state hidden in my robe."

But before my master could respond, and better hide the scroll he had accepted from our landlord, heavy feet thundered up the stairs.

The door was flung open, and a helmeted pikeman thrust his head into the room. The crested, highly polished helmet gleamed in the light from our lamp. He gave us a measuring look. Then he stepped back, and had a quiet word with a shadowy figure.

A man in a long, sea-dark cape stepped into the room.

Chapter
9

ANY LONDONER WOULD HAVE RECOGNIZED him.

All of us had seen Howard of Effingham, the Lord Admiral of the Queen's navy, as he arrived for one of his audiences with the Queen, plumed and silked in the bow of a royal barge. One of the most powerful men in England, he was renowned as a man who liked his starched collar and Flemish linen as well as any man, but who could plot a ship's course and trim a sail, too.

His cape was dripping with the rain that must have begun falling again in the street, and his high, flare-topped boots were beaded with wet. The plume on his cap was bright copper red, a long, sweeping feather that showed no ill effect from the evening damp. He kept one hand on the pommel of the rapier at his hip, and gave my master a correct bow in return to my master's own flourish-and-leg, a courtly act of homage.

"I know you by reputation, Doctor Perrivale," said the Lord Admiral. "You saved my predecessor's life when his own wife had given him up for dead, and it pleases me to meet you at last."

"Bring us a pitcher of your best Rhine wine, Nicholas," said my master, bowing his thanks to Lord Howard for this compliment. "And quick-red coals for our hearth."

Nicholas scuttled sideways, bowing and looking up through his eyebrows, his shadow lurching and following him out of the room. A pikeman at the door shut the barrier fast, and I heard the pike-butt strike the floor as the guard positioned himself at the top of the stairs.

Lord Howard approached the sickbed. He stood there, not moving or making a sound, while a spatter of rain crossed our roof.

At last he gave a long sigh. "Can he hear us?"

"The sick can hear, my lord," said my master, "within their sleep."

Lord Howard sighed again, and turned to study the rows of books on the shelf, volumes of the ancient medical authority Galen in Latin, and anatomies from Padua and Verona—diagrams of wombs and spleens.

"Who is this young man?" asked Lord Howard.

"Thomas Spyre, my lord, my most worthy assistant."

"But is he worthy of trust?" asked the Lord Admiral meaningfully.

"As I am myself, my lord," said my master.

Lord Howard sat down in our best chair. We all kept our silence as Nicholas and his wife, in a dazzling white apron still creased where it had been folded and stored against some great occasion, made a show of arriving with a silver pitcher and green-glass cups, none of them chipped.

Mrs. Nashe set a taper candle in the middle of the table, and cocked her eyes at each of us in turn as she poured the drink.

A lad brought a brazier of coals, placed them with tongs in our dormant hearth, and thrust kindling into the fireplace. When the landlord departed from us again we inhabited a chamber as fit as any in London—except for the sound of Titus Cox's shallow, rattled breathing from the sickbed.

I remained standing, as was proper, holding the chair courteously as my master sat down at the table in our second-best chair, the one twice mended with glue. William extended the beribboned scroll, and Lord Howard accepted it with no evidence of relief at recovering this state document.

"Master Titus was sick, shivering at our meeting this morning," said Lord Howard. "He told me it was a fever that came and went, as such cold-sweats will, and that he would be fit enough to sail with the fleet."

"Drake's fleet, my lord?" asked my master.

Lord Howard tilted his head to eye me in the candlelight. He was a ruddy-faced man, with gray salting his beard, and a white, heavily starched collar.

My master said, "If it please you, my lord, speak before young Thomas as you would any honest subject of our gracious Queen."

"Will Titus recover?" asked Lord Howard.

"If my lord will forgive me," said my master, "he is beyond my power, or even the command of prayer."

Lord Howard broke the seal on the document. The scroll fell open, exposing black lines of writing. "As you will have guessed, this is a commission naming our friend Titus to act as surgeon to Sir Francis Drake and his fleet."

My master paused in the act of pouring the wine. "We took it to be a secret of state, my lord," said my master. "I had no dream of what it was."

Lord Howard smiled for the first time, taking a drink from a glass cup. "It is a secret, believed in by many but known as a fact by few. Drake will sail within the week, to raid the Spanish port of Cadiz, and sack every ship."

Cadiz was a celebrated harbor, where the richest ships in the world found shelter. A grizzled sea scholar had once explained to me that the ancients, the Phoenicians and the Romans, had moored there in ages past. The words thrilled me. I put a hand on the back of my master's chair, and I could feel him tense with excitement, too, a shiver running through his body.

"Can this be true?" breathed William. In years past Drake had bled the Spanish treasure fleets, and set ports in the Indies alight. In his legendary ship the *Golden Hind* he had sailed around the world. But never had this great sea captain, the most famous Englishman alive, accepted such a daring command.

As I stood there in the dancing hearth light I would have given my life for the chance to sail on such a voyage.

"It's true, before God," said Lord Howard in a matter-of-fact tone, but unable to completely hide his own thrill.

He hesitated, and measured out his next words carefully. "It does seem, however, that Drake will sail without a surgeon."

Barely aware what I was doing—acting on an impulse—I bent to my master's ear.

I was amazed at what I was bold enough to suggest.

William turned to look at me, his gray eyes gazing up into mine in wonderment. And then he smiled, looking at once years more youthful.

He turned back to the Lord of the Admiralty. "I myself sailed as a young ship's surgeon, my lord, on the *Gillyflower,* out of Plymouth. This no doubt was why good Titus sought me out."

Lord Howard made no sound, his long golden plume making a graceful arc in the glow from the fireplace.

My master continued, "My lord, Sir Francis Drake can sail, his health and that of his crew well attended by two medical men."

I straightened, proud of the sound of this.

Lord Howard drained his green-glass cup. He said nothing further.

"My lord," continued my master, "our gracious Queen has no more loyal subjects than the two of us."

"The men I appoint," said Lord Howard at last, his manner softening, "will be required to take an oath."

"We are yours to command," said my master.

Lord Howard's eyes, bright with firelight, looked hard into mine.

An oath, a contract sworn before God, was an agreement no man would knowingly violate. I hesitated, uncertain in my soul what I was about to undertake.

"My lord," I said, my voice as steady as my master's, "I am your servant."

"If you accept this charge," said the Lord Admiral, leaning forward and lowering his voice, "you will be surgeon and surgeon's mate on the *Elizabeth Bonaventure,* Drake's flagship."

My heart leaped.

"And you will be something even more important, in my view." The Lord Admiral spoke in a steel whisper. "Some say Drake is the sunlit seaman, that he can do no wrong. Others say he is sinfully ambitious, that he will sail halfway across an ocean, risking men and ships, for a button of gold to further round out his already ample money bag. It is whispered that of the treasure he brings back to the Exchequer, as much as one-fifth or even one-third disappears into his own strong box."

He looked from one of us to the other.

"If you swear this oath," he continued, "you serve as doctors to a war-fleet. And you will, in addition, be my eyes and ears—secretly reporting, after all is done, to me."

I silently prayed that God, through his Son Jesus Christ, might fulfill my life-long dream of adventure.

"You will be intelligencers," the Lord Admiral was saying. He leaned forward, into the candlelight, to make his meaning clear. "You will be Admiralty spies."

Chapter
10

THE SINGLE SAIL ON OUR BOAT WAS SWOLLEN
with the wind, and her prow cut the dawn-gilded river.

Our pinnace, a ten-ton scout-boat, was fast. She carried
us down the River Thames, out of London, and past
Greenwich, where the officers of the Admiralty met to plan
for naval glory, and the dry dock where the storied ship the
Golden Hind was kept in state.

The three slender masts of this famous vessel, in which
Sir Francis had sailed around the globe a few years before,
were barely visible in the early light as our pinnace made
short work of passing the early river traffic. The high
waters of the evening before had receded with the low tide,
and the night's rain showers had fled before a strong wind
out of the west.

I had never seen my master look so happy, his satchel of
medical supplies stowed safely in a stout chest. "I was up
this early every morning on the *Gillyflower*," he was saying,
the breeze in his hair. My master was habitually a late-riser
these days, waking early only if an emergency called him

forth. "I stood on the deck and watched the dawn. I saw a mermaid one day in the sea swells, a bowshot from the ship—did I ever tell you?"

Three dozen times, I could have responded. But moved by affection for my master, I offered truthfully, "I never tire of hearing of your voyage."

"She was like a beautiful woman," he said dreamily. "But her skin was—"

An oysterman, squat in his floppy hat, called out a deep-voiced *halloo* from his homely boat, not in greeting but to encourage us in sailing so fast.

"I am filled with delight, Tom," said my master, "that you'll see for yourself what full sails and clear sky do for a town-weary spirit."

We had sworn a solemn oath of loyalty to both Her Majesty and to the Lord Admiral himself. We had vowed to watch and learn, as only a doctor and his assistant can, the nature of our famous charge, the admiral of the war-fleet, Drake himself. I knew in one corner of my mind that this sacred promise could violate that trust a patient should have in his physician. If Drake fell ill and in his fever babbled confessions, we were bound to betray him.

I had wondered, too, at our great urgency, hurried into a pinnace before the night was out with only the clothes on our backs. A hasty message was sent in the darkest hour of night to Martin Frizer, a doctor with chambers near Moorgate, and the round-cheeked physician, cowled and armed with a silver-hilted sword, arrived breathless at the summons. One glance at the ready-to-depart Lord Admiral, and an earnest plea from my master, and Martin Frizer promised to preserve the life of our patient Titus Cox "as God gives me the power."

I had not been able to bid farewell to dark-haired Jane, or give the chambers that had been my home anything more than a hurried backward glance. All was haste, a solitary rat darting across Fenchurch Street as pikemen escorted us through the night-stunned city toward a wherry that hurried us toward the Admiralty docks. My master had explained that Drake and the Lord Admiral were working fast to complete the fleet and sail before the Queen, who was more changeable than weather, could withdraw her permission for the voyage.

I gave none of this a thought now as our pinnace took on speed, her ropes taut, the cheerful seaman at the helm calling out that if we kept this pace we'd catch the *Golden Lion* on her course for Plymouth. Mudhens along the river bank scurried awkwardly, and a chalk white horse watched us pass, our wake stirring the reeds.

We were the sole gentle passengers on this ship, but there was a crew and a cargo, bales of straw packed into the hold, and small wooden kegs, each marked with a red daub I recognized as the Admiralty's insignia. These barrels were ranked in tight rows, and held tightly in place by the straw. There were so many of these kegs that the hatch could not be closed, and bits of straw spun off into the wind. I would have taken the containers to be rare wines, knowing that sailors enjoyed their drink whether land-bound or at sea, except that the barrels were double-lashed with new black iron hoops, thick and sturdy.

My master took a cup of morning wine with the vessel's

captain, a short-legged mariner with a well-trimmed beard. I asked a young man spreading a thick canvas over the hatch, protecting the kegs from the rising spray, what the nature of our cargo might be.

He laughed. "Such a cargo as could carry us well, sir, and carry us far, all the way into the sky." He extended his explanation by adding, "Such cargo as could turn us into carrion, sir."

At that moment the canvas flapped, a great, breathy thunder, caught by a sudden wind. The captain gave a great cry, and the canvas would have taken off across the river if I had not reached for it, fumbled, and held on.

I kept a grip on the edge, and stretched the canvas tight while a seaman tied it into place.

"Well done, sir," said the young man. He leaned close to me. "Our hold is stuffed with gunpowder," he said. "Black as hearth dust and packed tight in kegs, for the culverins and serpentines of the fleet."

I nodded, as though I quite naturally understood such matters—which in part I did. Culverins were cannon of great girth, made for lobbing shot high and far. Serpentines were long-barreled guns. I had seen—and heard—gunnery practice in London just outside Bishopsgate, the bronze and iron pieces primed and fired with volumes of blue smoke, and I had dreamed of firing such a gun myself some day.

But this was real gunpowder, not the stuff of my imaginings, and it was packed under our feet. "It's safely stored, I see," I offered with the air of a man who cares nothing for his own safety.

"Nothing in the nature of gunpowder is safe, sir," said

my new friend with a laugh. "I've seen a cask of new-mixed fine-grain blow up as soon as sunlight hit it. No, sir, you'd be wise to pray the straw doesn't heat up in the hold, and blast us to Gravesend."

It was true that decaying straw, like manure in a pile, can ferment and grow warm. But I doubted that this clean straw could flicker into flame. My skepticism was confirmed by the twinkle in my new friend's eye.

"I'll work hard to surmount my fear," I said in the dry tone I had heard my master use on men of heavy wit.

My new friend laughed again. "I'm called Jack Flagg," he said. "I've signed on aboard the *Elizabeth Bonaventure* as a gunner's mate." He was my age, with a youthfully wispy beard, like mine, both of us trying to compete with the full sets of well-trimmed whiskers sported by the older men around us. He was liberally freckled, on both his face and his hands, and his eyes were sharp blue. Bruises marred his lively features, especially around his left eye, and his lower lip was swollen. His knuckles were scuffed, his right hand puffy, and I wondered if this injury had caused him trouble, grappling with the canvas.

I introduced myself, and wanted to add: and I have cured fevers and picked a splinter from a gunner's eye.

Jack squared the long, tasseled cap he wore more squarely on his head and said, "We have both corn powder, coarse-grained, and serpentine powder, fine as sifted flour, but a gentleman like yourself is safe enough. It's the gunners who risk their lives, sir, not a scholarly surgeon's mate, such as yourself."

I had noticed that kind-hearted seamen in the tavern

often took an attitude toward me that was both respectful and patronizing. Respectful because I was the son of a gentleman, and assistant to a gentle doctor, and because I could read both Latin and English. But patronizing because they had sailed before the wind, ice-daggers glittering in the rigging, while I had been studying learned treatises on the varieties of vomit.

Jack went on, "I was sent to the arsenal to collect this shipment of powder, and make sure it didn't get wet."

I envied this young man, still unable to sprout a full beard and yet entrusted with such an important duty.

"I would have disembarked last night," he added, "but I had my wits knocked out of my head by a giant and three of his mates outside the Red Rose Inn." He lowered his voice and confided, "I cannot drink wine or beer without swelling up in a fighting mood."

This explained the bruises, where someone's right fist had found its target. And it further impressed me. This was a youth of spirit, already a man of the world. To further dampen my pride, I had stowed my rapier in a large chest, near the sea bag that held spare stockings and my cloak. Jack Flagg sported a seaman's dirk—a short, all-purpose knife in a leather sheath at his hip.

"But no doubt you have had many medical adventures," said Jack warmly, perhaps recognizing that his personal accounts had put me in his shadow. "You've certainly stuffed wounds with gun-wadding in your time, and sawn off limbs by the dozen."

I looked aft, to make certain I was out of earshot of my master, and lied. "I've cut off more legs than I can count."

"Have you then?" said Jack, his eyes wide with respect.

"Of course," I added, and as I spoke I reached out to a strand of rigging, fine-woven rope, to steady myself against the bucking of our vessel. It was not strictly an untruth. I had cut off none.

A voice called out from the helm, a husky bawl, "Hands off the sheets, sir," someone directed me, "lest you spoil her trim." Or words to that effect—the accent was strange to my ear and the sailing terms all but foreign.

Jack clapped a hand on the rail.

"Keep your balance," he said, with every show of kindness, "like this."

With spray in my eyes, I suffered the indignity of being shown how to hang on to a rail.

Chapter

II

●

THE TWO DAYS WE SPENT SAILING FROM
the mouth of the Thames along the coast westward to
Plymouth were celebrated by the crew of our pinnace as a
speedy voyage, and well favored by the wind. Before noon
on the first day we passed the *Golden Lion* cutting a pretty
wake but slower than our vessel. Her sailors called out
greetings.

For me it was a time spent seasick, so much so that I
found a place in the prow, and let the wind refresh my spirits. My master, too, looked pale as pudding, and he said this
was to be expected until "like old sailors we goat-foot
around the deck."

He was right—I was feeling hale and seaman-like by the
time we reached Plymouth.

The harbor was crowded with ships' boats and barges,
packet boats for carrying messages, and carracks for deliv-
ering freight. The warships themselves were packed close,

robust, brightly painted vessels, each ship a towering web of rigging, sails tight-furled. Rumor was that privateers raked the coast, legalized pirates of several nations. Merchants and fishermen alike had hurried into harbor, grateful for the protection of the Queen's fighting ships.

I tried to spy our flagship—and our famous admiral—but could make out little in the crowd of shipping. I had seen Drake himself once or twice before, from a great distance. His river-boat had been pointed out to me, a long, low vessel painted red and gold, with silk pennants fluttering, carrying the famous red-whiskered mariner to Parliament, where he served. I had remarked to myself more than once that we were alike in the coloring of our hair, an unusual carrot-bright hue, and that we both hailed from the same West Country moorlands.

Our pinnace, propelled by oars, threaded through the crowd of ships' tenders and shallops, vessels used to carry messages from shore to ship. The harbor was at first glance haphazard, frigates nearly tangling with warships. But soon a brisk pattern emerged, and by the time we glided toward the inner harbor what had seemed chaos now looked like a well-ordered hive, ships' provisions lined along the distant wharf, barrels being lowered into lighters—supply boats—and the sing-song of orders being called out in every anchored hull we passed.

We approached a vessel painted a dazzling black and white, the scent of fresh paint in the air. The *Elizabeth Bonaventure* was a big ship. She had proud castles fore and aft, but her appearance was sleek, her newly pitched rigging hanging dark and stiff in the gray afternoon. Her masts were festooned with flags and pennons, none of them stirring—except one.

This flag toyed with the wind, emblazoned with a red-winged dragon, its talons wrapped around the globe.

It was the crest of Sir Francis Drake.

Chapter

12

•

"HEAVE HARD THERE," A VOICE SANG OUT, "or she'll crush us all flat."

Hovering over the ship, and high above our pinnace, a wooden crane lowered a large crate. The load shuddered downward, shadow swaying. Through the slats of the crate, rows of cannon balls gave off a dull, leaden gleam.

"Saker balls," said Jack Flagg at my side. I recognized the pleasant smile he gave me, an expert showing off his special knowledge. "The saker uses smaller shot than most guns, although the falconets aboard this ship will fire the smallest shot of all, the size of pigeons' eggs."

My heart quickened.

I had, in years past, played at war with my friends among the pig-troughs and millponds, flailing away with a wooden sword. Now I doubted the wisdom of entrusting my life to such a fighting vessel. I gazed upward, my ears alive with the sounds of orders, quick-barked commands, and the rhythmic songs of men heaving, and heaving again.

A high-pitched metal whistling rose and fell, a sweet

but plaintive signal which I recognized from my own dock-side wanderings as a boatswain's call. I thrilled at this sour music, even as I hesitated, unsure how to clamber up the ladder of knotted rope that had been flung down to us.

"Come along, Tom," called my master eagerly, already up and over the wale of the ship high above.

I climbed upward, laboring, using the webbed cordage as a foothold, hand over hand. I slipped twice, and Jack Flagg reached back to help me.

My friend would have said something welcoming, or perhaps cheerfully challenging—his eyes were alight with friendship. But a ferocious voice demanded that if he did not stow every keg of powder in the magazine by dark he'd be "flayed alive and rolled in salt."

The gray-haired master gunner gave a wry smile, the corners of his mouth turned down, as though to soften his speech, but he made an unmistakable gesture: hurry! Jack vanished back into the pinnace at once, and soon the kegs were handed up and carried across by a chain of men, into the ship's hold.

It was all so strange to my eyes and ears, and so ripe with danger—from the powder kegs to the pikes carried by the soldiers—that I was afraid to make a move, sure that I would be impaled on some dirk or grappling hook. The gray-cloaked soldiers handed firearms down into the hold carefully. They were harquebusses—portable weapons made to be held against the shoulder, and discharged into an enemy.

As I watched, a load of shot, blue-black and round, broke free from a crate and struck a long, slim-barreled gun on the main deck with a resounding report. The stoutly built gunner let forth a bellow, and men scampered after the rolling shot, seizing the offending balls as they made their way heavily across the deck. The master gunner knelt beside the long-barreled gun and examined it carefully. He ran his finger along the seam where, at some point in the past, smiths had joined the two halves of this formidable weapon.

A dark-haired gentleman with a well-trimmed beard separated from a group of seamen. He took a coin-sized object from an inner pocket and held it in the flat of his hand, adjusting his stance to catch the sunlight. He returned the miniature sun-dial to his pocket and made his way toward us, eyeing us as he came, a smile of greeting fixed upon his face, his eyes alight with inquiry.

"I am Sam Foxcroft, the ship's master," he announced himself simply. "I'm just in receipt of word from the Admiralty regarding our newly appointed medical men."

William swept his cap from his head and gave a handsome demonstration of a courteous bow, and I was quick to follow his example. The ship's captain and William exchanged appropriate pleasantries, but I was aware of the captain's glance, weighing and testing us.

Captain Foxcroft was dressed much like my master, in a blue wool cloak and doublet, and high boots. "I am advised that our worthy naval surgeon Titus Cox is in need of our prayers."

"I have emptied many a cup of sack-wine with my good friend Titus," said my master. "In our university days we were rivals for a certain lady's affections," he added. "A lady of quality—she presented me with a hart-bone manicure set, I am sorry to report, but to Titus she gave a pomander filled with cloves."

Captain Foxcroft smiled at this. The clove was a spice celebrating love—it was used to flavor wine and to sweeten the air. "An old friend of Titus will be most welcome," said the ship's master, sparing me not another glance but explaining to William where the surgeon's quarters could be found, and adding, "We have two hundred and fifty men aboard a ship that can be worked by a score or less."

"We sail with a battalion!" said William.

Captain Foxcroft nodded, but he was already turning away, calling out orders in tart naval language.

Admiral Drake would not captain the ship himself, my master explained as we entered the shadowy interior of the vessel—those duties would be discharged by Samuel Foxcroft. The admiral would be free to contemplate military matters, and stay out of sight, no doubt with a chart and compass.

The interior of our ship was like the inside of a great wooden house, with many stories of pegged oak floors, ladders leading from one level to the other. Great cannon lined the gun deck, but wood-joints creaked all around, just like any city dwelling of timber. At times I could not stand upright below-decks—the ceilings were low and crossed with heavy wooden beams. But most of the sailors were short men, and scrambled easily through the badly illuminated living and storage places.

Our berth was a little chamber beneath the ship's aft castle, with shelves of medical supplies ordered some weeks past by Titus Cox. The surgeon's cabin was very small, but most dwelling rooms in London were little larger, a small room being easier to heat and keep tidy.

The ship's below-decks may have resembled a house, but they did not smell like one. Sulfur had been burned to fumigate rats out of the hold, and vinegar had been employed to cleanse the ballast—the stones in the ship's hold that kept her steady in the waves. And through the odor of new paint rose the permeating perfume of the salt sea.

My master examined his own bone saws before he hung them on hooks provided for just such items, the broad-toothed tools for large limbs, and the glittering whipsaw, the sort a chair maker might use—or a surgeon cutting a hand at the wrist. Titus's supplies included clay containers of spearmint syrup and others of dried mace, useful against lung diseases, and aqua vitae—distilled spirits—useful against pain. There was even a jug of opium-wine, my master noted approvingly. But he chuckled sadly when he took down an earthenware container and slipped off its wax-cloth lid.

A glistening, dark gray worm, as large as my fist, slowly felt its way along the mouth of the jug.

"Titus," said my master, "would never sail without his leeches."

Somewhere above there was a muffled crash. The ship shivered almost imperceptibly. A cry rose, an involuntary, wordless wail of pain.

From the hatchway came the scuffling, stumbling procession of feet as someone was helped, half-dragged, half-carried, down the steps.

Chapter

13

•

"DOCTORS, BY YOUR LEAVE," SAID A SAILOR, stiff with good manners. "If you please, sirs, a seaman has squashed his finger."

I always braced myself before I took in the sight of an injury, and I became quietly apprehensive now at the sounds as they approached—stifled cries of agony. His fellows were reassuring him, "The two doctors will see you right, Davy."

My master and I cleared a space on the pinewood table in our cramped cabin.

A young man, suntanned and bearded, gritted his teeth against the pain, blood flowing from a finger crushed flat. His fellows supported him, their weathered faces lined with concern. "Davy Wyott here suffered a great accident," said a seaman formally, as though describing an event many weeks past. "A heavy barrel of beer, if it please you, sirs, fell down upon his hand."

"I was helping to lower it into the hold," said Davy, pale

under his sun-browned complexion, "and the poxy rope slipped."

My master shook his head sympathetically, and bid the gathered seamen a good day—there was no room for so many concerned faces in our tiny cabin. When we were alone with our patient, William made a low, airy whistle. "You managed to splinter the bone, Davy."

The seaman laughed, through his pain, at his own bad judgment. "I thought I could carry the beer, but it carried me, all the way down, with only my hand between it and the planking." He chattered anxiously, adding, with a frightened laugh, "I've seen a sailing man die of a mangled finger before."

"So have we all," said my master. "We've watched injuries like this sour and poison many a strong young man."

"Before their time!" howled Davy.

"But we'll keep you in the world of the living, yet," said my master kindly. "Hold the injury still," said my master to me, moving the oil lamp closer to the bloody sight. The middle digit of Davy Wyott's left hand was flattened, blood bubbling.

To his patient my master said, "A quick blow with a keen edge, Davy, and you'll die an old and toothless mariner, many winters from now." To me he added, "A cup of spirits of wine, if you please, Thomas, for our brave patient. And the chopper from the hook."

The cleaver, he meant.

The blade gleaming on the wall.

Chapter

14

"IS THERE NO WAY," QUAILED OUR PATIENT, "to save the poor, mashed thing?"

My master gave a gentle smile. "My dear Davy, it's only one wee finger."

The patient drank down the amber-colored aqua vitae, a good quantity. I gave him a second serving, and he drank that straight down, too. "Merciful doctors, you are," he gasped earnestly when he had quaffed the spirits, "both of you."

I did my best to look kind and wise, but I never did like amputations. I had never performed one, nor did I want to—I had a particular horror of the sudden violence such operations demanded. My master spoke to me, partly in Latin to disguise our consultation, "The *sinistral ossa metacarpalia* as a whole is sound, Tom." The hand, he meant, was uninjured, except for the crushed finger.

"*Bene, bene,*" I said, trying to sound breezy and unconcerned. Davy nodded at the sound of Latin words—medical novices had been known to utter Latin-sounding nonsense to impress and reassure patients.

"Ordinarily," my master continued in slow-cadenced, calming Latin, "an operation would be carried out under the sky, where there is more space and light."

I was ready to agree that it would be hard to envision a more cramped setting. In clear, gentle English, my master instructed Davy to pray, and the patient echoed the words, his voice ragged.

"Almighty and merciful God," my master intoned, "extend your goodness to us, your servants, who are grieved and in great need of your love." It was the prayer my master always used at such times, and Davy followed along, his words slurring as the distilled spirits dulled his tongue.

At the final phrase, "with Thee in life everlasting," my master lifted the chopper.

"No, please, wait!" cried our patient, jerking his hand, my strength not enough to steady him.

"Fetch the mallet, Tom, if you will," directed my master in a whisper.

Where it was necessary, a blow to the head would render a patient unconscious. Doctors provided themselves with a wooden mallet for just this purpose, and I had used it on a few patients before—the task required a judicious touch in order to stun but not to permanently injure. I retrieved this hammer from the place where it was suspended on the wall, and Davy began to beg, "No, don't batter my skull, worthy doctors, please leave my head whole."

Distracted by the mere sight of the mallet in my hands, Davy was not watching the cleaver.

I never had to use the hammer. Davy screamed, half in pain and half in wonderment, at the suddenness of the chopper's blow. The poor wreck of a finger, no bigger than a chicken bone, fell with a chime into the basin.

Chapter
15

●

AFTER THIS VIVID ADVENTURE IN MEDICINE,
I was surprised to see that we were still snugly in port, having voyaged nowhere.

I glanced around for a glimpse of our famous admiral. Everywhere I saw shipboard bustle, but no sign of the legendary Drake.

I had never seen any city except London, and had expected Plymouth to be a sleepy port, with peaked roofs in a row. But even from the wharf it was plain that this was a town with taverns of the rougher sort, dung heaps up and down the meandering streets, lean cats scrambling out of the way of staggering sailors.

The *Golden Lion* had arrived at last, nosing her way toward the wharf, and every seaman and officer knew that this was a night to drink and sport, because at the next ebb tide the fleet might take us to sea.

"Are you hungry, Thomas?" asked my master as I followed him. He surveyed the crowded, muddy by-ways of this port, wondering aloud which doubtful, smoky lane promised the best food. A dust-colored tom cat observed me from a coil of hemp rope, but when I reached to scratch his head the cat hissed.

We had left Davy Wyott at peace with the world because of the drink he had swallowed, a ship's boy in attendance, spirit-flask nearby. I was very hungry, and thirsty, too. But when I saw two seamen wrestling each other in a puddle, surrounded by cheering crewmates, I asked my master's leave. I hurried back to the ship, into our cabin for my sword, and my master's blade, too.

"Only a seaman dare sup or drink in Plymouth," said Jack with a wink, sitting on the deck of the ship. He was pulling on his boots, and had put on a new cap, with a red feather. Such feathers are pretty, but dyed. A golden fighting cock's plume—a color ordained by nature—angled from my own hat.

"A gentleman like you," said Jack with a laugh, "even with a sword, will be a fawn among lions, if you'll forgive me."

I offered Jack our protection in return, with what I thought was a manly laugh. "So if you find yourself in rough company, we can save your skin."

"A rapier is not a cleaver, by God," said Jack. "Or a surgeon's mallet, either."

I had noticed glances of interest and, I thought, respect from our shipmates. Talk of our capable treatment of Davy Wyott's injury had evidently spread.

My master and I found an inn called the Mitre and Parrot.

We dined there on mutton, hearty slices of it, hot and

served on slabs of brown bread. We drank a thick, sweet beer, and were soon content.

We sat with our feet before the fire, and my master told me in detail of the mermaid again. It was a story I had come to love, if only for the mood that came over my master when he spun the tale. Sometimes called *meermaids* or *merewives*, these sea-sirens showed themselves as a special favor to men of character. To see one was a sign of great good luck, and to hear one speak a rare wonder.

"She had long, streaming tresses," he reminisced, as often before, "and dazzling green skin."

He paused, no doubt seeing her again in his mind. "She looked right at me, Tom, as sure as I'm a Christian. She parted her lips and she spoke." He shook his head. "By the time I called to the boatswain—a good fellow, but slow-footed—she was gone."

It was my part, now, to ask the question I always did at this point in the tale. "What did she say to you, my lord?"

He gave a thoughtful laugh.

My master's mind was a quilt, skepticism and critical reason stitched neatly within seemly faith and prayer. He had taught me that the representations of eyeballs and hearts in the expensively printed books were "fanciful, no more like real organs than a puppet is like a man." The only way to learn, he had taught me, was to question. At the same time, he often surveyed the star charts before an important operation, believing that a retrograde Saturn or unlucky moon could slow a patient's recovery.

When men at a nearby tavern table rattled a dice cup

and called out, "Who'll share a wager?" my master gave me a pained smile and shook his head.

"We are new men, now, aren't we, Tom?"

When we agreed that we could eat no more—and not, with any wisdom, drink any more beer—we stepped out into the street. It was dark, except for a few pitch lamps, and we made our way down toward the harbor.

"The mermaid said my name that morning," said my master, continuing his tale much later, now that we were free of the tavern's din. This part of the story had great meaning for him, and he did not like to speak of it lightly. "She spoke my Christian name. *William*. Very clearly pronounced."

"It was a powerful omen," I said, as I always did.

Usually, the story having been told, my master entered into a happy discourse on such omens, and praised astrologers at the expense of mere magicians—men and women who read the future with the help of the mottles on a sheep's liver. Astrologers read the stars, and were quite respectable—every royal court had at least one.

But this night my master did not expand on the stars and their mysterious powers. He took my arm and said, "Listen!"

As we entered the domain of cats—the entire parish having an acrid, feline scent to it—we heard the grunt and gasping of a fight, booted feet striking a body.

A familiar voice cried out for help.

Chapter
16

•

MY MASTER STRODE FORWARD, CALLING out, "Enough work for one night, gentlemen rufflers— leave off."

A *ruffler* was a vagabond, a humorous, wryly mocking term. My master approached four figures. Two of the men were armed with clubs—knobby, ugly lengths of wood— and two more looked on. They were jeering, plumed fellows, rapiers at their hips.

The squirming, injured figure at their feet stirred, gasping for breath. He looked up at us in the dim light.

At once I put my hand to my hilt.

The victim of these brutes was none other than my friend Jack Flagg. Red blood flowed hard from a gash in his nose, and Jack's eyes met mine. He parted his lips to beg our help—or to warn us away.

The street-brawlers drew their rapiers, each with a flourish I had to admire. I regretted in that instant that fencing tutors, and zeal for the art of swordplay, were common throughout our kingdom. Every ale house had its one-eyed sword master, wise in the ways of cold steel, and happy to impart ability to any student with a purse.

My master had his sword in hand, and he made a good show of knowing how the thing should be held. But the bone saw and the chopper were my master's true weapons, and he could no more cut a true circle in the air with his weapon than take wing across the star-splashed sky.

My master certainly looked capable, however. There in the darkness, the puddles gilded with the light from pitch lamps and candles, William engaged the attention of the shorter and slighter of the two swordsman, while I took my fighting stance against a tall, heavily built man with high boots.

Teachers are common enough—but good teachers are treasures. Giacomo di Angelo had told me that if I followed his lessons, drilled into me by months of sweat, I need fear no man.

My opponent was evidently used to the cut-and-thrust school of sword-work, dashing my blade aside, lunging for my upper thighs and groin, where even an inaccurate attack could be painful and crippling. This brutal attack surprised me—before now all my supposed enemies had been fellow students, careful to avoid causing injury.

If you would strike fast, my teacher used to tell me, you must strike straight. I thrust at my opponent's right knee, desperate to disable him, but he blocked my lunge with ease. I knocked my enemy's blade down and away, kicking at it with my boot. He nearly dropped it, and I closed on him, striking him hard on the temple with the hilt-end of my weapon.

The muscular swordsman collapsed, sprawling, puddle-water quaking around him. I knelt briefly, to make sure he was still breathing, and then I rose and strode hard into the man attacking my master. I kicked this stout street-fighter hard, right in his padded breeches. He howled, and turned and closed upon me at once, scissoring one leg through mine, trying to drive me into the wet street. We teetered, and fell, and as we struck the wet street a loud snap echoed from the surrounding eaves and chimneys.

We both leaped immediately to our feet. I knelt and plucked a sword-half from the ground. To my surprise—perhaps out of some dim, misguided sense of honor—I found myself handing this length of broken rapier back to my sweating opponent.

"Ah, you're a true penny," he panted, sarcastically. "Break a man's sword and expect him to smith it new."

I made a bow, ready to recommence our struggle.

To my surprise—and relief—he laughed. He struck me on the shoulder—hard, but with an unmistakable air of good-natured retirement. He and his fellow townsmen dragged their friend from the puddle, and vanished up a side street.

"You're a pair of fighting doctors, by Jesus," Jack addressed us shakily as I helped him out of the mud. "I am beyond thankful to see you."

"You fought with your face, by all appearances," I said, sorry to see my friend so badly battered. My master was quick in dabbing at the bridge of Jack's bleeding face with a linen kerchief.

"There's a woman in the tale," said Jack with an air of

jaunty regret. "She wanted silver, and I had been led to believe that her interest in me was true love. I protested, and with no further ado she called her brothers or her father, and a gang of pirates. They would have killed me." He sniffed. "I cannot drink and keep from fighting."

But then Jack fell silent.

A man in a padded doublet and jerkin that made him look massive strode down upon us through the dim lamp-light, splashing puddles with his boots. He was a constable, outfitted just like the lawmen of London. He sported a high-peaked, broad-brimmed hat and stout dark gloves that stretched nearly all the way to each elbow. Instead of a sword he carried a mace, a spiked knob on the end of a short staff, a symbol of the law's authority—and a potentially deadly weapon.

"Gentlemen," he called after us, "save your fighting humors for the Spanish."

Chapter
17

●

I WOKE IN THE *ELIZABETH BONAVENTURE.*

The vessel was a noisy, exciting place at such a time. Feet pounded along the deck over our heads, commands were called out—"Quick, there!" "Heave with a will"— and other shouted orders I found more mysterious than Dutch. My master was pulling on his boots, and swallowing a cup of wine, his usual breakfast.

He wished me a good morning, with a heartiness I had rarely seen in him before, and hurried out of our cramped cabin. His boots resounded on the companionway—the steps from one deck to another—as he ascended into daylight.

I caught a glimpse of myself in the polished metal disk my master and I used as a looking glass. My red hair was *elfed*—tangled into the knots and curls folk say is the work of fairy-like creatures in the night. I did what I could with my appearance, knowing all the while that seasoned fighting men would be observing me that day, judging whether I would be a capable shipmate or not.

A trumpet sang out.

I thrilled. The tune was a traditional call, something I had only dreamed of hearing, a signal to all the ships in the fleet. *To sea, to sea.*

I felt the scrape of the boat, and the welcoming greetings, as the harbor pilot arrived. I climbed on deck, blinking in the sunlight, as Captain Foxcroft gave out commands in an even voice, and a mate sang them out in turn. A chant accompanied much of the work as the ship turned, alive in the water, and we began to make our way.

"Isn't it a sight to bring joy, Tom?" said William.

It was indeed. Sails followed us, the *Golden Lion,* with the rest of our fleet in her wake. William Borough, the vice-admiral, sailed on our sister warship, a man with a reputation for clever navigation and stubborn quarrels. Captain Foxcroft gazed back at the warship in our wake. Harbor collisions were common in every port, and tides sometimes shifted shoals that troubled the progress of vessels.

But we were safely away.

A crisp wind blew, and every man with a rope to knot or a gun to secure was hard at work—the swells were strong enough to loosen anything that was not fastened tightly. Spray lashed the air, and the masts and rigging groaned under the press of canvas.

We were a trim fleet, but smaller than I would have expected: several warships, seven or eight merchant ships recently outfitted with guns, and a scattering of smaller vessels. Ale-drinking mariners had expressed the opinion in my hearing that as many as forty Spanish ships might crowd the harbor of Cadiz, with war galleys and armed galleons primed to defend them. Our own ship was fortified by a whiskery set of soldiers, who even now polished their breastplates and began to be seasick. It would not be a short journey. The Atlantic port of Cadiz was over one thousand English miles from home. We would skirt the western shores of France, and the coast of Portugal, as we sailed south, all the way to Spanish waters.

The wind continued fresh. We soon began to leave the *Golden Lion* and the rest of the fleet far behind.

We were a crowded ship, but every man had a task. The seamen in their plain gray slops—a mariner's ill-fitting garments—contrasted with the brightly colored jerkins of the sergeants, and the plumes of a few gentlemen who had evidently joined the force.

I kept a sharp eye on the quarterdeck where Captain Foxcroft was directing the crew. Surely soon, I thought, the famous sea-knight would make his appearance.

But as yet I caught no glimpse of Admiral Drake.

Chapter
18

TO MY SURPRISE, DAVY WYOTT CALLED AN energetic greeting. He waved a heavily bandaged hand from a yard arm above, where he worked with his fellow sailors. I had heard that mariners were as tough as boxwood, and now I began to believe it.

I gave a wave in return, and found Jack Flagg leaning into the spray, setting his feet with a practiced air against the liveliness of our ship. I staggered, unbalanced, and would have fallen if he had not held out a strong, callused hand. I would have asked my experienced new friend how such a small navy might weigh in against the best Spanish ships, but I was afraid of exposing some new ignorance in myself.

Jack's nose was scored across the ridge with a cut that might well leave a lasting scar, and one eye was swollen. "They teach young doctors how to use a sword," said Jack, for the benefit of his mates.

Jack's master was a thick-set man called Ross Bagot, the gray-haired gunner I had seen the day before. "The rapier," scoffed the master with a friendly dismissiveness. "It's a pretty but trifling weapon."

My pride stirred, but I kept my silence.

"Let's show Tom here what our guns can do," Jack implored his master.

His gunner responded by turning down his mouth, an upside-down smile that indicated a decided negative. But at the same time the veteran's eye twinkled. He cast his gaze upward, eyed the empty blue sky, and made his way aft to the place where Captain Foxcroft and my own master William were in conference, each gentleman eating a slice of white bread.

It was easy to mark the progress of the conversation that followed, the gray-haired gunner seeking permission, the captain considering. William joined in with excited pleasure, gesturing toward the guns on the main deck.

Most of our ship's cannon were arrayed on the gun deck below, the gunports closed tight against the heaving of the sea. A few of the more slender, pretty weapons gleamed on the main deck, however, and Jack Flagg was giving one of these cast-bronze guns a possessive wipe with a fine white rag.

At last the captain gave a nod of assent.

We were well out to sea, the fleet trailing far behind, England already a receding shadow of land. The morning sun was warm, but in the shadow of mast and sail the air was bitterly cold.

I stayed beside my master, both of us just out of the way of the gunners. "Something about the whiff of gunpowder,"

William was saying, "has always set my pulse beating fast. How about you, Tom—don't you love a great noise?"

I had seen the bombards fired on feast days, and reveled in the amounts of smoke the cannon made. In truth, I had always considered myself a young man who loved the reports of such war engines, along with drums and the minstrel's pipe.

But this morning I felt the slightest fever of anxiety, some ill-humor quickening in me, and making me wish for calm and quiet. I didn't want to dampen my master's boyish joy in anticipating the gunfire, however. "Nothing, sir, pleases me so much as a deafening noise," I joked, my feet planted wide against the restless sea.

The long, narrow gun I had observed the day before—the one that had nearly been damaged in an accident—glinted brighter than ever in the sunlight. The master gunner fed the round opening at the end of the barrel with a carefully measured amount of blue-black powder.

Jack used a long wooden rod to tamp this powder into place, and then forced a wad of cloth after it, running the rod in and out. A small shot, no bigger than a quail's egg, was set into the mouth. So closely did this ball fit the circumference of the barrel that careful effort was required to force it all the way down. The master gunner himself tapped the rod home to satisfy himself that the gun was well charged.

"The worst thing in a gun is windage," my master explained to me knowingly. "That's the space between the ball and the inside of the gun. Too much windage and the shot flies feebly."

"If the gentleman would be pleased," said Ross, giving my master a nod. He indicated a smoking wick, held by one of the mates, a smoldering, glowing stub of knotted fiber the man blew on to keep alive.

"It would please me," said William, "if Tom here would be allowed the honor."

Ross Bagot looked at me with a ponderous dignity, a glimmer of good humor in his eyes. "Are you sure this young gentleman," asked the master gunner, "is equal to the task?"

"Anything I could do," said William, "young Thomas here could do with the same steady hand."

The master gunner smiled.

I hesitated, like anyone of good sense, before such a momentous act. But I did not stay my hand for more than a heartbeat or two. I accepted the glowing wick, and heard the gunner's instructions even as I braced myself for what I knew would be a very loud report.

But then the gray-haired gunner gripped my arm.

He hissed into my ear, "Stand straight!"

Feet shuffled as an air of respectful quiet—even nervous fear—swept the men. I stood as squarely and calmly as I could, my eyes searching for the cause of this sudden alarm.

A gentleman in a scarlet doublet gazed down at us from the quarterdeck.

He surveyed us for a long moment.

He wore a closely trimmed red beard, and sported yellow kid gloves on his hands, a gold-knobbed sword at his hip. Many of the men had seized their caps from the deck and thrust them onto their heads, a show of respect. Every one of us recognized Admiral Drake, and I sensed that each of us felt caught in the midst of some unready act.

Captain Foxcroft hurried up the steps to the side of his lord. We could all see his greeting, and hear, in our respectful hush, the word of explanation. "The surgeon's mate, getting a whiff of gun smoke, Admiral, if it please you."

The Admiral Drake looked right into my eyes. Perhaps he remarked to himself the similarity in our coloring, both of us with the same red hair. He gave me a smile. This pleased me greatly, and I stood as straight as any man on deck. Then he took us all in with another glance before he spoke in a quiet voice.

I caught the sound of Admiral Drake's words, his accent like the folk of my home town near the River Tavy. "Yes, Captain Foxcroft," he said, "give the men a taste of black powder."

"Touch it into the hole, there, in the breech of the gun," whispered the master gunner with fresh excitement. "Now, young sir, if it please you. Right in there," he added fervently, pointing with a gnarled, big-knuckled forefinger.

Not me, I wanted to protest.

Just then—with the storied sea-knight looking on, and every other crew member on the ship casting their eyes my way with envy and anticipation—I could not move.

William leaned toward me. "Come on, Tom—it's as easy as kiss-the-duchess," he said with a wink.

I hesitated, blowing nervously on the glowing wick. Jack Flagg smiled and rolled his eyes. I was grateful for the good humor of his mock-scowl: hurry!

I stepped forward, wasting not a further moment, and I thrust the glowing wick into the touch hole.

I held my breath.

Nothing happened.

I thrust the wick in farther, all the way in, my knuckles on the cold gold-brown bronze of the gun.

Chapter

19

•

THE NEXT MOMENT, I WAS LYING FLAT ON the wooden deck.

In my surprise, I did not know why I was there. High above me loomed the mainmast, a sail billowing with the breeze, rigging taut and black against blue sky. I puzzled out what must have happened.

A sick fear gripped me.

I was coughing by then, the thick stink of sweet-acrid sulfur in my nostrils. I tried to lift my head but I could not control the sinews of my neck and arms. Even my eyes were failing me, stinging with the smoke. Jack was kneeling beside me, and seamen gazed down at me, their features creased with concern.

I was nearly deaf, too, even as I struggled onto one elbow, and worked myself to my feet, Jack helping me. I read the words on his lips, but even then took a shaky moment to comprehend.

An explosion.

A gun had burst. *The* gun, the one I had fired.

I understood this all now.

I put my hands to my head, reassured to feel my skull in one piece. Jack was beseeching me to tell him if I was hurt badly. I could not answer, upright on my weak, unsteady legs. Like a drunkard far gone in wine I pieced together what I would say, some weak jest, as soon as I could move my lips.

I groped across the deck through metal fragments that my hands and booted feet struck and knocked aside, bits of what looked like a bronze bell shattered and strewn about the planks. I did not know fully what I sought, or what person. I felt my way through the thick, parting smoke, and fell to my knees beside the stretched form of my master.

I seized his hand and rubbed it, to work life into his pulse, as I had seen done by William himself in reviving a patient suffering a swoon. I tugged at his arm, and spoke, my voice muffled and strange in my own ears.

I implored him to speak to me.

Hands stretched out, other men coming to my aid, but I did not have a glance for them, or a thought. I bent down over my master hearing my own, foreign-sounding voice like a sound from many fathoms down, calling for him to look at me. I begged him to turn his eyes and look into mine. I put my hands on his chest, and on the pulse points of his neck, but my senses were too unsteady to be trusted, a ringing sound in my ears.

My master's unseeing eyes were unmoving, his limbs slack where he sprawled on the deck. His pupils were fixed and wide. A fragment of dark bronze was fixed in the center of his forehead, a ragged star shape of metal, a fine trickle of blood threading down, across his temple, to the wooden planks.

Ross Bagot put a hand out to me. I was beginning to be able to make out sounds as Captain Foxcroft joined him, his steps causing subtle vibrations in the deck. The captain addressed me solicitously, words I still could not hear clearly. The smoke had been driven clear by the wind now, and I wondered which of these men to send for medicines, vinegar to splash on my master's face, spirits of wine to awaken his tongue.

I caught the eye of a ship's boy, a wide-eyed lad with hair the color of straw. My voice was heavy, my words sluggish, as I directed the lad. "Bring me the doctor's satchel from the shelf."

The boy stared. The captain murmured something to the child, and he scampered off. I leaned over my master and slapped his cheeks. I told him we'd see him right, and very soon, too, imitating the manner and speech William himself had employed during similar crises.

The ship's boy hurried back with my master's satchel, and I found the lancet and bleeding cup within. I would open a vein and drain a cup of blood—a sure remedy for a host of emergencies.

Like many fighting ships, our vessel had a man of God on board, a straw-haired man with a wispy yellow beard, with no ornament to show that he was a cleric. With every show of prayerfulness this man knelt beside me. I was grateful at the sound of Our Father, in straight-forward prayer-book English. Christ Jesus would aid my master's recovery.

I was confused, too. More than confused—the prayer

awakened me to a feeling of inexpressible uncertainty. The chaplain offered a prayer for "our departed shipmate," and I felt an unsteady surge of anger.

My master was not dead, I wanted to protest, and it was unseemly in the extreme to pretend that he was. I put out a hand to silence the chaplain, and Jack Flagg put his arm around me, despite my protest, saying, "Come away, Tom."

I struggled.

The chaplain and my friend the gunner's mate were both misguided. My master could look to me for good judgment. I would open a vein, release the dark humors that had captured my master's senses, and he would be sitting up and asking for a cup of rhenish wine in no time at all.

"On deck there," sounded a clear, commanding voice that cut through the ringing in my ears.

The captain, the gunner, and all the present ship's company on the main deck straightened immediately.

Admiral Drake leaned over the quarterdeck rail and gave the order, "Take the surgeon's mate into my cabin."

Firm hands seized my arms.

"And Captain Foxcroft," the admiral added crisply, "look to the ship."

Chapter

20

•

I SAT IN AN OAK-PANELED CABIN.

Pewter flagons perched on a shelf, held in place by a restraining rail against the movement of the ship. Rolled-up charts peeked out of leather sleeves, sepia coastlines marked with dark brown writing. A compass was fastened to the tabletop, set within a box and kept steady by gimbals, brass pivots that secured the compasss against the motion of the swells.

A ship's boy brought a pitcher and poured cider into one of the flagons, a large drinking vessel with a hinged lid, and set it before me.

"Admiral Drake sends his best compliments," said the lad, my hearing improving with each heartbeat, "and begs you await him with good cheer."

Despite my numb senses, the fact that I was about to have an interview with the great sea fighter made me apprehensive. Was I going to be blamed for the accident with the gun, and its consequence? William would be very angry with me, when he recovered.

The lad left me alone with my disordered fears. I would be accused of some felony, and spend the voyage in chains, my future among rats. I made no move to drink, although I kept my hand on the flagon to keep it from skittering off the table.

I stood at once as Admiral Drake entered the cabin.

His cheeks were ruddy, flecks of spray even now soaking into his brightly colored doublet. He unfastened the rapier from his waist, and set the weapon on the floor. He motioned for me to sit, but I would not.

He poured cider from a silver pitcher and drank.

"He's dead," said Admiral Drake.

My ears were still ringing somewhat, but I could make out his speech, and indeed the subtle sounds of the ship all round, clearly enough. The admiral's words, however, carried no meaning that I wished to take in.

The admiral continued, "We'll have the prayer book service for burial at sea this evening, at the set of sun. It is a pity. He was a good doctor, and an honest man by every account, but now he's gone to God."

I kept my mind a perfect blank.

"You understand me, don't you?" said the admiral in a gentle but probing voice.

"I need to go to him," I heard myself manage to say.

"Your master is killed," he said, "as you must know. The gun burst into pieces. It's rare but not unheard of. A fragment smote him, and you will not serve him anymore."

His accent was very much that of the Dartmoor neighbors of my boyhood. *Yew-er mauster iss killt.*

"I know far more about medicine," I said, forgetting every courtesy, "than any of this ship's company." I was immediately ashamed of myself for speaking so bluntly to this great man, and I silenced myself.

"It delights me to hear it," said the admiral. "But your master is with Jesus."

Each heartbeat hammered this tidings into me. I looked away. I closed my eyes and opened them again, perhaps hoping that this ship's cabin, the vessel, would prove a mere nightmare.

"Then," I rasped, "I must go back to England."

"How?" he asked.

"In one of the ship's boats," I said. "A pinnace, perhaps."

He gave a gentle laugh. "Thomas, you will voyage with us."

"But with no master to serve—" I faltered.

I wept, then, wordless, a breaking of my soul that left me baying like a beast for a long while.

When I could speak again, I heard the admiral's gentle command, "Take a sip of good cider, Thomas. And sit down."

I did sit, and the admiral joined me, pouring himself another serving of golden brown cider. I could not keep from noticing that he handled both the pitcher and the flagon a little clumsily, using his gloved right hand sparingly.

"Sir, I will go home," I insisted, taking a swallow of this strong, warming drink.

"And leave my ship without a surgeon, Thomas?"

"I am no surgeon, my Lord Admiral." Despite my great grief I was clear-headed enough to employ proper courtesy.

"If I say you are a surgeon," said Admiral Drake, "then you are one."

"I know too little of green bile," I protested, "or the dangers of excess phlegm, or the right quantity of aniseed for curing fever—if that is what it's for."

"A surgeon bleeds the feverish," said the admiral, "cuts off the blasted limb that offends the body's health, and gives strength to the uneasy soul." He leaned forward. "We are two red-haired men with accents much alike, and I'll wager you, too, have a preference for cider over beer."

"I like beer as well as cider—" But I recognized the truth in what the admiral was asserting. Our cider is a bracing fermented drink, and West Country apples are renowned.

"Your family must have lived near mine, Thomas."

"I was a boy in Moreton."

"Not a day's walk from Tavistock," said the admiral, "where my family fished the river and milked the cows for many a year."

"I know," I said truthfully, "that every hamlet of Dartmoor is proud to be associated with your fame."

"We're two fellows who waded the River Tavy," said the famous knight with a brisk good cheer. "And I'll not see you turn into a coward over the death of your good master."

Coward or not, I wanted to respond, my own honor did not matter to me.

"Do you think your master is the last man you'll see dead within the fortnight, Thomas Spyre?" continued Admiral Drake. "We're voyaging to singe the beard of the king of Spain, right into the harbor of Cadiz. There we'll burn everything we can set spark to, and you'll see Spanish blood. It will run down the decks. You'll win glory and perhaps a few *reals* of Papist gold. And you'll be surgeon of this ship, or I'll set a knotted lash to your back."

"If my patients die, my lord," I persisted woodenly, "if they sink away and lose their lives under my care, sir, the fault is yours."

To my great puzzlement—and perhaps my relief—the admiral laughed. "Thomas, surgeons do little to save a man's life. What a doctor knows about the ways of breath and bone could be written on the side of a thimble. Our Lord Jesus cures us, or takes us, as he chooses. You'll be as sound a doctor as any under the sky, or I'm a goose."

To my further surprise I found myself wryly smiling through my tears, understanding at least a part of the admiral's ironic view of my profession. "Because you have such a low opinion of medicine, you know I'm equal to the challenge."

"I'll have the sailmaker stitch you a scholar's hat," he replied, "a floppy one, the sort philosophers wear when they dispute the weight of the moon's shadow."

I could not keep myself from laughing, despite my grief. "My Lord Admiral, dressing me like a learned gentleman will not make me one."

"It will," said Admiral Drake, "if I say it does."

He spoke with such a spirit of self-assurance that I was dazzled—and very nearly convinced.

"Can you set a splint?" he asked with a smile.

"I have done it, sir."

"And cauterize a wound?" he continued, his bright, steady eyes on mine.

Many doctors advised searing an injury, especially gunshot wounds, with a hot iron. My master had taught me that cauterizing did more harm than good. "My lord, if you desire it."

"Tell me, Thomas—how old are you?"

I recalled then my vow to the Admiralty in London, swearing that I would spy on this great Englishman. Such a promise could not be lightly broken. It would be an advantage to my mission to stay on as surgeon.

"My lord," I said, adding more than three years to the truth, "On the next anniversary of my birth, I shall be twenty-one."

"Old enough," he replied with satisfaction.

I felt a dash of my own pride, and a spirit of my own that prompted me to ask, "My Lord Admiral, is your gloved right hand unhurt?"

He withdrew his hand, and placed it below the table.

"Why," he said, "do you ask?"

Chapter
21

•

BEFORE I COULD RESPOND, A DISTANT CRY reached us, a call from a mast top.

"Sail, off the port beam," I thought I could make out—the nautical phrasing was both foreign and dimly audible to my ears.

"Thomas," he said, his cheeks flushing, "we'll see if we can't pluck a few fat hens." He left the cabin, cradling his gloved right hand in the other.

He returned at once with Captain Foxcroft, the two of them in rapt conversation. The vessel the lookout had spied on the horizon was no doubt well armed, the captain was saying. More important, our fleet, including the *Golden Lion*, had been left behind by our rapid progress, and scattered by the increasingly heavy weather.

Captain Foxcroft hesitated to say more in my presence, but the admiral waved his yellow-gloved hand impatiently, and so both men continued a discussion laced with naval jargon. The admiral could order the ship's master to sail in any direction or circumstance, but some courtesy made the sea-knight take pains to explain his commands.

"If we voyage alone, what does it matter?" concluded Admiral Drake. "We'll teach our enemies that God fights for Her Majesty on the high seas as well as on land, or any heathen shore."

"May it be so," said the captain with little heart.

Captain Foxcroft accepted a flagon of cider, and then studied me for a long moment as he drank.

"I am making Thomas Spyre here," said the admiral briskly, "our new ship's surgeon."

"There is logic to the choice, Admiral, it might be said," said the captain after a long moment. "I have heard that he can handle a sword."

"So if he cannot cure," said the admiral with a laugh, "then God grant that he can kill." He had a way of rising to his tiptoes for a moment to emphasize certain statements, and his cheeks colored, as I am told mine do, with feeling.

"But forgive me for suggesting," the captain continued, "that this surgeon's youth argues against him. We have Sir Robert Garr on board, a playwright and scholar of seven languages, who wrote that famous poem about the liver. He has cured fevers with his knowledge of stars and planets—"

"Thomas is older than he looks," said Admiral Drake. "And he is from the West Country moorlands—a place that breeds canny men."

"I've seen evidence of that," said the captain, with the faintest trace of a smile.

"Sir Robert," said Drake, "wrote a play about John Hawkins, called 'Knight of the Something Something.'"

"'Knight of the Ocean Sea,'" said the captain. "It was quite good, by my reckoning."

"The speeches were badly metered," said the admiral, "the swordplay childish—I did not like it." John Hawkins was a well-known sea fighter, and Drake had sailed with the storied captain early in his career. Drake had become far more famous. "I know Sir Robert studied medicine and alchemy and can brew poison from a dried scorpion—but he's not in good health."

"We could wait for the *Golden Lion* to come up," said Captain Foxcroft. "No doubt the vice-admiral could spare us a medical man."

"The master surgeon of that ship," said Admiral Drake, "is a man pickled in wine, with a mate little better."

"Vice-Admiral Borough," said the captain, with a courteous smile, "is a good friend of mine."

"And a stubborn man," said Admiral Drake, "sailing— as God has willed it—on a creeping-slow ship."

The captain parted his lips, to defend his friend or counsel caution, I did not wait to hear which.

"If the admiral will permit me," I said, putting as much maturity into my tone as I could muster, "to attend to his own injury, I would be grateful."

"I wear this kid-skin glove to protect a hurt," Admiral Drake said when we were alone, "as you have guessed."

"May I examine your wound, my lord?"

He tugged the fingers of the glove, wincing, and stretched his hand before me, palm down.

"If it please you, sir." I tenderly turned the hand over,

and moved the lamp from the side shelf to the tabletop.

The inner ball of his thumb was swollen, angry, and I could easily spy the cause.

"Some splinter has lodged here," I said. "And it gives you grief."

"An armorer tried to sell the Queen's navy a few score bill-hooks," said the admiral, pepper in his voice. "Halberds with a protruding blade, for ship-to-ship fighting. We'll need such weapons, and very soon."

To hear this famous sea-knight mention battle brought a thrill to my heart, despite my stricken spirits.

"The shafts of the weapons were some whoreson wood," the admiral continued, "nothing like the fine-grained ash they should have been. When I tried one out, battling with a sergeant, the poxy thing broke in my grasp."

"I'll tweezer it out, with your consent—"

He smiled, his storm-blue eyes narrowing.

The ship's boy brought my master's satchel.

"What is your name, lad?" I heard Admiral Drake ask the boy as I searched among the steel and bronze tools.

"My lord," said the boy self-consciously, "I am called Hercules."

"And was some ancient Greek divinity your father?" asked the admiral.

"Hercules Biggand is my name," said the boy, surely no older than six or seven years. "With your permission," he added.

"Stay here, lad," said the admiral, "and hold this lamp

for the two of us, while our ship's surgeon drags a spear from my skin."

Hercules had a steady hand, and his help was necessary to keep the motion of the ship from shifting shadows. I bent close.

I questioned my skill as I sat there in the sea-rocked vessel, mariners barking orders beyond us on the deck. I knew well that surgery was difficult enough in a quiet city, on a steady floor in my master's chamber. Shaken by feeling, and a newcomer to medical practice, who was I to undertake even a very minor operation on this great seaman—on board an increasingly unsteady war-vessel?

I tried to imagine what my master would have advised, but instead I heard the lesson of my sword-teacher.

If you would strike fast you must strike straight.

One instant, and the splinter was withdrawn.

Chapter
22

"THEY HAVE ONE LITTLE SAKER, THERE IN the prow," Jack Flagg said.

He was indicating an indistinguishable glint on the distant ship as we approached. "They'll have a few more guns covered over with sailcloth," he added.

"Hidden?" I suggested.

"Making their peaceful intentions clear," said Jack.

He hesitated, and then he added, "The seam in the gun was weak, as nobody could have known."

I did not have the words to weigh my feelings just then.

"When that cannon sundered, Tom," he continued, his voice hoarse with sorrow, "my heart stopped dead in my body, and I doubt it's started beating again. You're in my prayers."

I thanked him, strong feeling choking my speech.

"I have a token for you," he said. He stretched out his hand, and into mine placed a barbed claw-like thing, a talon, it seemed, carved of wood. I closed my grasp around it, gingerly, aware that this was no common gift.

"It's the fighting spur of Pepper John," said Jack. "The best rooster to ever draw blood on the Southbank. I traded a hanged man's knuckle for it. It's yours, Tom, and may it bring you luck."

I wanted to protest. This gift was too gracious, and too valuable. How could my friend load and fire war-engines if he was stripped of every charm against ill-fortune?

Jack and I fell silent as a mariner relieved his bladder in the piss-barrel nearby. The big containers were kept tied to the ship's side in case of fire—nothing damped a blaze like urine. Fire was a great threat on a sailing vessel. One of the most potent weapons of sea battle were the legendary fire-ships, vessels packed with pitch and set alight, and set forth with the wind in their sails to ram and destroy enemy craft.

A soldier vomited down his stockings before he could reach the rail, and a muffled cry rose up from the galley, where rumor had it the cook was having trouble keeping his great copper stock pot on the fire. And then the master gunner called for Jack, and I realized, as my friend hurried off to attend to the guns, that there was little time for heart-to-heart conversation on a warship.

A mariner's song flavored the breeze as men climbed the mainmast to work the softly thundering sails.

We captured a Flemish carrack that afternoon, a stocky little merchantman with two masts and gold paint about her stern.

Her sailors hauled the ship up out of the wind, and

made no attempt to flee or fight as we approached. Our pikemen stood by with gleaming points at the end of their shafts, some of them armed with a weapon called Welshhooks, a stout staff with a long sharp bill at the end. Gunners stood by, wicks at the ready, giving off soft feathers of smoke.

Our purser and his mates climbed aboard the *Sint Joachim* to inventory the bales of wool and the barrels of medicinal spirits, supervising the wrestling of the cargo up and into our own hold. When all was done, in the space of an hour or two, the Flemish sailors waved farewell and set sail for the east, apparently relieved to have come so close to the famous sea fighter without loss of life.

I felt relieved, too—that the first act of war I had ever witnessed was a matter-of-fact act of plunder, carried out with efficiency and an air of mercy. If this was sea battle, I thought, perhaps I would live to see England again.

My master's body was committed to the sea before a sunset blotted by clouds. The mortal remains of William Perrivale, worshipful Latinist and gifted physician, were sewn into a swaddling of sailcloth weighted with shot.

The yellow-bearded chaplain hunched into the sea spray whipped through the air by the rising wind, and protected the leaves of his leather-bound book with his mantle. I knew the prayers, even though I could not utter them out now as the chaplain recited them in the rising storm. I wept as never before in my life.

A few sailing men and gunners attended the service,

and Captain Foxcroft and the admiral were present, but I understood the pious brevity of the prayers, and the continued activity as men worked the ship. Shipboard death was mourned simply, and was far more common than I had imagined.

As the chaplain closed his prayer book, and the last eddy of foam coiled over my master's remains, someone touched my shoulder.

Chapter

23

•

I WAS GRIEVED BEYOND TEARS BY THEN,
and welcomed contact from my shipmates, but this man's
physical appearance stilled my tongue.

I had glimpsed his bright plume among the crew, but I
had not seen him face-to-face before this, and never with his
expensive cap removed. This gentleman's head was bald,
and he sported flowing mustachios, but what disturbed me
about his appearance was the tint of his skin. He embar-
rassed me by uttering some patch of Italian—Petrarch, I
suspected—and he apologized at once in gentlemanly
English when I could not respond in kind.

"I show off my learning the way a bawd shows off her
dimples," said this tall man in a civil manner. He gave me a
hand to help me stay upright—we were both swayed one
way and another by the spirited seas. "I am Robert Garr,
and I used to take a cup of wine or two with Titus Cox.
That worthy doctor used to mention your master as a great
friend."

"You would have found my master the best man under

Heaven," I said, and then I had to silence myself, close to tears again.

Sir Robert gave a sympathetic sigh.

I realized that it was not simply the ashy light of the dying day that gave a strange tint to his features—Sir Robert had in truth a striking and unusual coloration. His skin, his lips, and the moons of his fingernails, were all the same off-hue. This well-known knight and poet was blue.

He was not bright blue, but the dusty cloud-blue of a fresh bruise. It was a medical symptom I knew from William's consultations with a few unfortunate scholars in London. Sir Robert's condition was the result of quicksilver poisoning.

The mercury that learned men used in their studies seeped into their flesh over months and years. In unlucky instances, it turned them this unholy tint, and in some star-crossed cases it even drove them mad. Many philosophers dabbled in alchemy, believing that base metals could be turned to gold by using quicksilver and other rare elements. Sir Robert's condition was striking, but one shared by other seekers.

"Captain Foxcroft whispered a word in my ear," said Sir Robert. "Something about taking you under my wing, if you seemed in need of my help."

I bridled inwardly. The admiral had chosen me to be one of the ship's officers, and I was determined to live up to Drake's faith in me.

"Not that I suspect you'll need any special advice, good Thomas," said Sir Robert with polite haste.

"We are lucky to have such a spirited shipmate," I offered, liking him despite my stung pride. "You are a well-famed playwright and poet, as I hear."

Gentlemen scholars were often carried on a ship, and were expected to work the vessel and to fight, when the occasion rose. Such men of letters helped fund the voyage with fat donations, and with any luck would survive to write a glorious history of the vessel.

He gave a quiet chuckle. "The truth is, I wrote my heroic poem 'The Liver in Her Glory' when I was but twenty years of age, and I am much fallen from my former knowledge."

"I regret I did not attend a performance of your play," I heard myself say smoothly, like any gentleman in a London wine-shop. I appreciated Sir Robert's honesty, and relished a chance to talk with such a learned man. In my sadness, I remembered to converse as my master had taught me, trying to be both kind and truthful. "I've heard little but praise for it," I said. It was nearly true.

"Oh, I can't pen a good line of ten-syllable verse to save my life," he said. "The play was all speeches and sallies. Sword fights, you know, actors running on and off stage in red stockings."

"I do wish I'd seen it," I said, sincerely.

"Look, Captain Foxcroft is watching us."

The ship's master was indeed looking on, his arms folded as he stood in a corner of the quarterdeck. The strong wind stirred his mantle.

"Let us pretend that I shall act as your advisor," said Sir

Robert in a gentle tone, "just to deceive our worthy captain."

Perhaps I hesitated, because Sir Robert added with a smile, "Good Thomas, I shall do nothing to offend you. I am dying from the elements I have brewed and bubbled in my study, as you see. I hope to be killed after I've sent a hundred enemy to the Devil."

Chapter
24

•

"DO NOT SET A CUP DOWN, SIR," HERCULES instructed me patiently, "unless you have finished drinking from it."

I would forget, and my cider would spill, knocked over by the plunging of the ship. In weather so heavy we ate in our own quarters, stock-fish—mummified cod—and ship's bread of rye and wheat, along with apples and pears, and all the beer or cider we could pour into our bellies.

Every knife seemed alive, and nothing remained where I had put it down. Jars lost their pewter lids, and flasks tossed on their shelf.

"Have you been to sea before, Hercules?" I asked.

"Oh, yes, sir, on the *Mountjoy,* which sank."

"She was shipwrecked?"

"She was a much used wine-ship and rotten, and off Ostend she went down."

This was a great tale to be offered in one breath, but it certainly increased my respect for Hercules.

"You will tell me next," I said, "that you sank to the

bottom and drowned, except some hero saved you."

"No, sir," he said in a matter-of-fact sing-song, "a ship's boat took us off and we were preserved, except for those who died."

"Are many children taken to sea?"

"Sir, the Admiralty pays our parents and we learn the trade of seamen."

I was shaken by the sudden death that awaited every mortal on a warship, and wondered that children should be so exposed to danger.

"Besides," Hercules was saying, "being small we fit the crowded ship life, if it please you."

I asked how old he was. Hercules confided that he had seen eleven winters—I had reckoned him very much younger.

"And now that I am a surgeon's boy," he continued, "some day I'll grow to be surgeon's mate, and, if it please the Admiralty, some day I may set splints and drink my wine spiced, just like a gentleman surgeon." He caught himself, and put a hand out to a chafing dish that was dancing its way across our tabletop.

"Unless I'm wrong, sir," he added questioningly, "to dream of such things?"

Our ship crashed into seas over the coming days, the admiral commanding the captain to crow on canvas, and the mariner who was manning the whipstaff—the device that worked the vessel's rudder—was often thrown off his feet by the force of the waves.

Even as I mourned my master, a succession of drenched

and shivering seamen limped into the surgeon's cabin presenting dislocated shoulders, hobbling sprains, and black eyes where tackle had broken loose and smashed into the men trying to secure it. The cook himself, a stout man with tufted eyebrows, presented a broken thumb. The stubborn stock pot had once again leaped from the sputtering fire—"cold soup all over my knave of a galley-mate." I set a splint, and was entirely sincere in wishing him the speediest recovery.

Our first shipboard patient, Davy, his hand bandaged, often accompanied the injured with praise and reassurance, recounting how his finger had dropped into the waiting bowl with "a merry note, like a little chiming bell." He showed the mangled digit to his friends, suspended in a green-glass jug of spirits of wine—my master had long emphasized the keeping of specimens.

Days passed, wet and cold, with no sign of our fleet.

Jack Flagg confided to me that under any other officers the crew might have been apprehensive, but under Admiral Drake, "We would sail singing 'hey-ho' into the teeth of Hell."

Later I would wonder if my friend had some gift as a prophet.

Chapter
25

●

LATE ON THE AFTERNOON OF OUR TENTH
day out, a cry came down from our top castle, the viewing
platform high on the mainmast.

"A sail, dead ahead!"

I made my way to the main deck and joined soldiers and
seamen in gazing out over an ocean alive with white caps
and wind-foam, clouds parting and showing feeble blue for
the first time in several days. As before, there was no sign of
our fleet to our stern. The ships had been scattered by days
of hard weather; although Jack had confided that the
Golden Lion had been seen "hull up on the horizon, when
the rain parted and the wind took a breath."

Now a sail tossed on the gray seas ahead of us as men
tried to guess her nationality and cargo. She was a good-
sized ship, Jack murmured, and the admiral paced the
quarterdeck, rubbing his hands together.

All the rest of that day our ship gave chase to this mysterious set of sails. The weather was heavy, and while it filled

our canvas and drew us ever nearer to this unknown ship, the stranger made every show of not wanting to be caught.

Intercepting a privateer—a ship licensed to intercept merchant shipping—would win us her stolen cargo. Even better, the chance capture of a Spanish galleon, blown off course by this bad weather, would earn us all a share in gold from the New World.

A chase at sea, however, is nothing like a foot race, all over in the space of a few heartbeats. Hours would pass, and the fugitive ship would be only a slightly more vivid ghost on the sea far ahead, like a drawing an invisible artist was limning in, sail by sail, mast by mast. Even by the following dawn the vessel was merely a pretty phantom, still far out of range of even our most powerful guns.

But our soldiers took their morning beer-and-biscuit with a determined air, and as the weather grew more calm the pikes were handed around, and sword belts were shaken out and buckled on. Some of the pikemen powdered their hands with resin from a bucket, the sticky, chalky stuff whitening their fingers.

It took a long time even now to work our vessel into range, and a sleepy unreality had by then turned the chase into a story-tapestry unwound so slowly and so haltingly that the tale would never reach its end.

And then, by late morning, it began to end after all.

The strange ship was very much closer now, as we approached her from off her starboard quarter, rapidly closing the gap. The invisible artist had sketched in rigging and yard arms, tackles and the fine woodwork decorating her stern. A thread of smoke drifted from her hull, rising up around her in the wind.

"She's English," Sir Robert offered in a matter-of-fact tone. "And a merchantman—by my guess a wine-ship."

I asked the knight how he could be sure of her nationality. He explained. "Her sails are unpainted. The Spanish love crosses and lions on their canvas. And look at the prow, how simple it is, not like a galleon's great painted beakhead, sticking out over the front of the ship."

We shortened the distance even more, the merchantman not able to continue to sail with anything like our speed. "She's English without doubt," said the knight, "and she's been in a fight—look at the loose rigging where some attacker has cut it, and the powder burns around her gunports."

Our own guns were being primed, and Jack bent over the breech of a long, golden-bronze piece on the maindeck, giving the weapon an affectionate pat. Our larger guns, on the gun deck below, had been forged with decorations, lion faces and roiling dragons, and gunners had worked hard to keep this bestiary gleaming.

To my surprise our ship flags and pennons, including Drake's personal insignia, had been hauled down, and replaced by Flemish colors.

"Master surgeon," came the call, the admiral's voice. In my distraction, and unfamiliarity with my new duties, I did not respond at once, not until the captain had joined in, barking my name.

"Be ready to board the ship, as soon as she's our prisoner," said the admiral with purposeful smile when I had hastened to his side. "I know this vessel, the *Barbara Grace,* a cargo ship out of Southampton. She's run across pirates, by the look of her."

"We'll nose gunpowder soon," said Captain Foxcroft. "Some fool is double-cracking the merchantman's stern gun." Ramming a double charge of powder into the rear cannon, he meant, and Admiral Drake gave a laugh.

"This," said the admiral, "will be greater sport than I'd hoped."

A tiny human figure at the stern of the merchant ship crouched low over the stern gun with its bronze-green barrel. The report of the cannon followed by several heartbeats the flash of smoke and the sight of a shot skipping fast across the water. It crossed the sea before our bow. A few other men, tiny insects at this distance, opened gunports and ran out the round mouths of cannon.

The *Barbara Grace* vanished in the sudden burst of gun smoke, and shot screamed overhead.

Chapter 26

"OPEN THE GUNPORTS, CAPTAIN FOXCROFT," said Admiral Drake, quietly, like a man requesting another pitcher of cider.

Perhaps the captain hesitated for one moment. But then he strode, smartly enough, to the quarterdeck rail and sang out the orders.

Archery screens were arrayed now over the sides of our ship, and wood and linen screens were set up around the guns. Even more screens were being put into place between the cannon on the gun deck, when I took a glance below. Called *fightings,* these shelters would protect the guns from sparks thrown off by adjoining weapons.

I evidently could not disguise the alarm I was feeling, because the admiral took one measuring look at me and laughed. "Wear a smile, Tom. This is the lively conclusion to a merry chase."

When I nodded speechlessly, wishing I shared his high spirits, he added, "The *Barbara Grace* is defended by a prize crew—men left to work her ashore and strip her of every penny's-worth. We don't care to risk sinking her, because there are probably hostages below-decks."

"Are these Spanish pirates," I asked, "or perhaps Portuguese?"

"Neither, Tom," he said. "Our English pirates are the foxes of the sea."

We swept down upon the *Barbara Grace.*

Our serpentines—long, narrow guns—fired over our prow as we got within smelling distance of her. And she did smell, as a random breeze swept back in our direction. Many ships had a strong odor—the ballast souring in the hold, human residue pooling in the crannies, old salt fish and seaman sweat combining to give every evidence of humanity to the wind.

I thought that firing on the rear of the merchantman was an unlikely way of harming a ship, but the admiral himself told me that the stern of a vessel is usually her weakest point, and that a well-placed ball could "pierce a captain's larder and turn him to suet."

Perhaps the archers in our mast tops caused confusion, sending arrows far out and over the *Barbara Grace,* hitting something on the deck more often than not. Certainly many arrows were loosed, and our archers threw taunts after them.

But at last we ran up our true colors, including Drake's own personal insignia. I think it was the sight of these, fluttering from our mast tops, that crippled our enemy's resolve. The fighting men of the *Barbara Grace* soon made every show of surrender, waving scraps of sailcloth, lowering every ensign or flag she once sported. The merchant vessel turned aside to wallow forlornly in the wind.

At once a boarding party was formed, the sergeants ordering the soldiers to arms. Every man, it seemed, used coarse language, "whoreson" and "poxy." No one said "God damned," however, or used Christ's name in vain— Admiral Drake was famously devout and disapproved of shipboard blasphemy. No one mentioned the Devil either— certain bad luck at such a time.

I went down onto the maindeck, striding along with an assurance I wished I had truly felt. The seamen wore their long baggy breeches of gray or blue cloth, and the soldiers dressed like fighting cocks in crested helmets, bright red or yellow sleeves, and gleaming metal breastplates.

Our ship drew alongside the cargo ship and nudged her, a gentle collision but solid enough to cause the rigging to shudder. The mainmast of the *Barbara Grace* swayed, and at that moment I was sure the pirates would resist, their surrender a ruse.

These English pirates were hard-looking men, outfitted in gaudy jerkins, shot-scarred breastplates. One or two wore long mantles, the sort knights and lawyers wear in wet weather, although slashed and tattered. Their weapons, which they made a great demonstration of throwing down upon the deck, were mostly cutlasses, a broad-bladed chopping sword, along with every variety of knife.

"Admiral Drake, sir, do you remember me?" one of the pirates was calling—a man in yellow stockings and a quilted red doublet. He searched the outline of our ship hopefully, not seeing the famous commander, but calling out again,

"Do you remember me, Admiral—we sailed together, under Captain Hawkins. It's Rice Catton, my lord, at your service."

Our admiral leaned out over the quarterdeck rail.

"You remember me, my Lord Admiral, if it please you," sang out Rice Catton, his voice trembling now with a blend of fear and hope. "We look to your famous mercy, Admiral, if God will quicken your heart to grant it."

Admiral Drake gave a frowning smile, most chilling to see.

Chapter

27

WE CLAMBERED DOWN A TACKLE-STAIR—A gangway of knotted ropes—into the smoke-grimed vessel. I managed to make my way without falling, although Sir Robert gave me a hand as I half-stumbled onto the deck.

The sunlight made his skin hue all the more unearthly, that faint but quite evident twilight blue permeating his flesh. Of course, such a physical abnormality would not go much noticed among sea-faring folk, a breed of men afflicted with wens and goiters, scars and boils. Sir Robert strode among the silent, sullen enemy, every inch a knight ready for blood, challenging them to give him an opportunity to use his sword.

But each pirate used the same, fervent cry, kneeling, hands together as though already bound. "Quarter, merciful quarter," they begged. Admiral Drake had a name as a man who struck fast against any who opposed him, but used a gentle hand toward those who surrendered.

"This way, doctor," panted one of our soldiers in my ear. "There's a brace of gunshot men."

I hurried. The prize crew pirates were thrown down hard, pressed flat against the bloody deck by booted feet, and challenged to stay still. Swords were being stacked into a heap of glittering steel, and daggers and bodkins joined them, the tossed weapons clattering. Firearms were stacked, too, ugly, wide-bore guns.

The stricken men were near the foremast. There were two, their chests charred by powder burns and punctured by heavy-weight gunshots—round, gaping wounds. They had been mariners, judging by their gray, loose-fitting breeches, and were beyond my help.

"We've found ladies," sang out a voice as I knelt, offering a prayer for these departed souls.

A murmur swept the boarding party. "By God, master surgeon," said yet another soldier, blaspheming out of Drake's earshot. "There's two ladies on board, and one of them half killed."

The interior of the ship was even more cramped than our own.

The smoke was heavily flavored with tar, and I coughed as I waded through it, led on by one of the sergeants. Some of our soldiers had found the source of the fumes in one of the after-holds, a barrel of pine-pitch they smothered with sailcloth.

At last I came to a cabin in the stern where two of our soldiers were kneeling outside an open doorway. The barrier had been smashed, splinters of white wood strewn everywhere.

I peered within the room, and immediately withdrew my head in an effort to preserve my life.

A young woman with a large pistol primed and leveled stood within the cabin, a second woman sprawling just behind her.

"Madam, I am Thomas Spyre, of London," I said, my voice weak with shock. "By God's grace, and our admiral's mercy," I continued as handsomely as I could, "I am an officer of Her Majesty's ship *Elizabeth Bonaventure*."

The two soldiers gave my little address encouraging smiles and, I thought, appreciative nods. Brave, well-tooled speech was much admired throughout Christendom—or so my master had taught me. I could not stifle a stab of regret that he was not here to prompt my words.

"I am surgeon under Admiral Drake, Madam," I continued, steadying my voice, "and I seek to uncover any injury done to you by these pirates."

This last was spoken with a degree of spirit—it angered me that cruel, greedy men could put a crew of innocent seamen and two women in such danger.

I thrust my head once more into the doorway, and once again looked into the green eyes of the young woman. She gave no evidence of weakening, the pistol cocked and steady, her gaze boring right into mine. One twitch of her finger and I would be killed.

I offered her a hopeful smile.

She was well favored, the very likeness of a graceful young woman, dressed as English women did when they traveled, in a linen cap and hood and a bodice that tapered to her waist, all in a soft blue that would show little wear or soil on a long journey. The woman at her feet was older, similarly dressed and handsome, her breath labored, like someone whose passage of air is not clear.

"I pray you," I said, "let me attend to the injured woman."

The ship made a groan around us. Cargo was being hefted out onto the deck, and I heard the clipped tones of the purser, giving commands to his mates.

"Only you may enter, entirely alone," said the young woman. "And if you displease me in the least way I shall discharge this pistol through your head."

"I would desire my own death, by my faith," I said, "if any harm should befall you."

The truth was, despite my flowery speech, I was hoping only that this beautiful Amazon put down her weapon, and let me save the life of the injured woman. Prompted by this professional desire, I found myself in the cabin, kneeling by the side of a stricken female passenger, moving her head to one side so she might breathe more easily.

"Will my mother awaken soon?" the young woman was asking.

The weapon was held loosely in her grasp, now. It was all the more dangerous for that, aimed in no particular direction. Her finger remained on the firing catch, the *tricker,* a little lever under the stock of the weapon.

"The good lady is breathing more easily now," I said, able to offer no more reassurance than that.

She had suffered a blow to the forehead, a bruise there

betraying the outline of a cutlass pommel. Her pulse was very feeble, but regular. When I examined her eyes, both pupils contracted to small points. I had seen enough people knocked flat in tavern brawls to recognize a woman who was stunned rather than mortally injured.

"Please, doctor," the young woman was saying, "preserve her life and I will reward you nobly."

No request had ever so captured my attention.

My patient blinked her eyes as I tried to loosen her clothing. Her eyes grew wide as I pondered the mystery of her bodice, trying to unfasten her clothes. My gentle patient knocked my cap away and grabbed two handfuls of my hair.

And screamed.

Chapter

28

•

I ANSWERED A SUMMONS TO THE ADMIRAL'S cabin that evening.

Drake and Captain Foxcroft were standing before an unfurled chart. The admiral's cheeks were flushed, and the captain leaned heavily on the table. A navigator's compass, two tapering points of brass, kept one corner of the chart from rolling up.

"How thrives your patient?" asked Admiral Drake.

"As before, my Lord Admiral," I said. "She is still convinced that I am a pirate." I tried to make light of this, but her addled insistence that I was about to do her violence concerned me greatly. The ship's carpenter and his mates had erected a cabin for the two ladies below the gun deck, a cramped space in an already crowded ship.

I had bathed her face and arms in vinegar, despite her stubborn disrespect for me, claiming that if she could get her hands on so much as a pin she would prick out my eyes. In her calmer moments she swore that her husband would have me clapped in irons if I harmed her or her daughter—

whose name, it appeared, was Anne. Head injuries are difficult, and I wished to keep her as calm as possible.

"She will live?" asked Captain Foxcroft pointedly.

"With our prayers being answered, my lord," I said, "she may even grow to bear the sight of me."

"Have you consulted Sir Robert?" asked the captain. His fingernails were gnawed to the quick, and his lips blistered with the sores that afflict people of anxious humor.

"That worthy scholar has not offered me his medical advice this day, my lord," I said. I desired only to return to my patient—and to Anne. "Besides, the good lady is in no very great danger." I silently prayed that I was right.

"We rely on our young surgeon," interjected the admiral quietly.

Captain Foxcroft gave a proper nod, almost a bow, but his gaze locked on mine.

Admiral Drake made a point of offering me a pewter flagon of cider before I could speak further, and continuing, with an air of boyish exultation, "Thomas, we have discovered why the *Barbara Grace* ran so hard before us."

"She was a floating wine-cask, my Lord Admiral," I said, a fact every mariner and soldier on board knew. We had helped ourselves to a few barrels of the better claret, as judged by the purser.

"More than that, she was carrying gold," said Captain Foxcroft, kicking an iron-braced strong box with his boot.

The chest had been opened by force, the lock twisted, gold coins spilling out onto the floor, gold marks and angel-coins, and other minted treasure. Several other strong boxes sat stolidly beside the ruptured chest.

"A wine merchant's life earnings," said the admiral, "sent north to England at an unlucky hour."

"Along with two women of good name," I said.

"Thomas, you would make an excellent privateer," said Admiral Drake with a smile. "I can see it in your eyes."

"Captain," I said, "I fear you have injured your foot." Just now, kicking the iron-edged box—Captain Foxcroft had been too proud to grimace, but his lips were white.

"I'll not put a further strain on your medical knowledge, Thomas," said Captain Foxcroft.

Anne Woodroofe and her mother, Mary, had been returning to England, the admiral explained, sailing from Bordeaux, where her father managed rich wine warehouses. Joseph Woodroofe was a man I knew by reputation, an importer of good drink, his name enough to make a good cup of wine taste even better. The worthy merchant had guessed that war between England and Spain was in the offing, but had foreseen it falling a year or two from now. He had not reckoned on pirates.

"I am deciding," said the admiral, "whether to pursue the pirate vessel herself, just to teach her a lesson."

The outlaw prize crew had been locked in the depth of the *Barbara Grace*'s hold, thrown hard onto the slimy flint-stones of the ballast. This was considered merciful treatment—many commanders would have hanged them at once.

Informed rumor had long recounted the belief that a good portion of the Queen's treasury was the result of Drake's past plunder of Spanish shipping. But where there was success, there was envy—and whispered doubt. Lord

Howard had sworn me to spy on the admiral's handling of such matters. I was anxious that the famous knight would prove deserving of my respect—and growing loyalty. But I wondered how honest he would prove to be.

"I pray, my lord, that we'll engage in no further fighting," said Captain Foxcroft, "until we can consult with Vice-Admiral Borough."

Drake responded, "Her Majesty did not appoint me to be toothless."

Chapter

29

"THE WOUND IN MY HAND HAS HEALED,
Thomas," said Admiral Drake when we were alone, waving my attentions aside. "I wanted some time alone with my
fellow west-countryman."

I found his attentions, and his confidence in me, both
flattering and encouraging, but I was aware that Captain
Foxcroft was no simpleton. Our famous admiral had more
faith in God, and in himself, than I could readily share.

"You'll see Spanish gore in Cadiz in less than a week's
time," the admiral was saying. "If the wind favors us—our
ship alone or with the fleet, it does not matter."

His decision to attack our great enemy so soon did not
give me joy—I was wiser than I had been that morning. I
had heard an enemy broadside howl over the mast tops, and
I had seen gunshot corpses.

I examined the admiral's hand in the light of the lamp.
It was, in truth, healing well. "Captain Foxcroft, my lord,"
I offered, "wants only to preserve his ship."

The admiral's glance was steady.

"But we shall all fight for you," I said, hastily, "and die, too, if you ask it."

The admiral made an expression of mock surprise. "I believe you attended performances of Sir Robert's play, Thomas, by my faith."

"No, my lord."

"It was larded with speeches like that," the admiral said, wincing theatrically at the memory, "paint-faced mariners stumping across the stage, waving false swords and spouting, 'Honor and glory, to our very deaths.' The knight could write well, if he was well inspired."

I knew very little about plays and poetry—in my ears the phrases the admiral had mocked sounded very fine. My expression of puzzlement must have spoken for me. The admiral drank off his flagon of cider in a good-humored show of patience.

"We'll fight and triumph, Thomas," said Admiral Drake at last, with a laugh. "And *live*," he emphasized. "And we'll sail home richer men."

At that moment I came close to confessing. I wanted this man with his ready laugh to know that I was a spy—I could not bear the burden of deceiving him. "This gold, my lord, will be returned to the Woodroofe family," I said, not a question so much as an assertion.

He raised an eyebrow. "Have you seen how well clothed our soldiers are, Thomas, all silk-slashed sleeves and bright colors?"

"A proud sight, my lord."

"Do you think Her Majesty can afford to pay for such fine stuff?"

The question had a certain weight. I did not know the answer.

"Sir Robert paid for our soldiers' clothing," he said. "He bought their armor, too—he has important friends in the Admiralty. In return he purchases a chance to cross swords with an enemy."

"I admire the learned knight, my lord," I said, because in truth I had found him a ready friend.

"Our Queen sees an approaching war with Spain," he said, "and she has little money."

I considered this.

"How much of our new-found gold," prompted Admiral Drake, indicating the strong boxes, "would the sea-robbers have returned to Joseph Woodroofe?"

"Not a farthing," I said, pleased to know the right answer, but at the same time feeling an illusion evaporate.

"Worse," said the admiral. "The wine merchant would have to borrow money to buy back his beloved wife and beautiful daughter."

"So we take a bite of the treasure, as our reward?" I asked weakly, feeling a degree of chill in the air.

"Thomas, you astonish me," said the admiral, screwing up his face in a show of being shocked. "We give the treasure, and any other plunder, entirely to the Queen. She takes what she requires."

"Forgive me, my lord, but our gracious Queen is—" I lowered my voice to a whisper, because what I was thinking was pure treason. Much like a thief, I would have said. But pamphleteers had suffered their hands cut off for publishing criticism of our monarch, and critics of God or Her

Majesty had found themselves tortured in Bridewell prison. Besides, if a fighting man steals for his queen perhaps it isn't really theft.

"This treasure is the Queen's to keep," said the admiral, "if she so desires."

I felt chastened, and much lost in the choppy waters of monarchs and God, about which I knew little.

There was hurried conversation at the door, and a guard stepped in, accompanied by Hercules.

The lad stood, waiting for my permission to speak, but I was so unused to having servants or assistants of any kind that the admiral himself had to prompt Hercules. "Use your tongue, boy."

"Our patient, if you please, sir," said Hercules, his eyes wide, "is dying!"

"Why did you leave us so long, Thomas?" said Anne. "My mother is worse than ever before."

I had no ready reassurance, out of breath and shocked at this turn of events, barely hearing Anne when she added, "I speak to her, and she doesn't even stir."

Hercules was pale with apprehension. "She puked yellow, sir," he said, "into the basin."

When I felt for my patient's pulse, her hands were moist and cold. Her heartbeat was a broken thread, unsteady and easily lost. I offered Anne my most soothing tone, telling her all would be well.

But I wished that I could be so certain.

"In London," Anne responded, "my mother is attended by Sir George Saltash, the author of 'The Moon in Her

Many Humors.' That worthy doctor gives her Virginia tobacco smoke to warm her blood."

Tobacco, as it is sometimes spelled, can be a useful drug. Blown up the nose, this newly discovered herb can wake up a gentleman knocked senseless, and I have heard it praised as an evacuator of the bowel. But I made no remark, rubbing Mary Woodroofe's hands. When I peered into her eyes, one pupil was a tiny pinprick, and the other dilated wide.

"Run quick and seek Sir Robert Garr, good Hercules," I said, keeping my voice as calm as I could manage, "and ask the scholar to pay us a visit, if he would."

My master had explained that an injury to the head causes fluids or vapors to build within the skull. Some medical men keep drills, with hard steel bits, for releasing the evil within the head.

That sort of surgery was beyond my scope. My patient struggled once again to breathe, and I knew I could not delay any longer. She was close to death.

"If you would reassure me regarding your schooling, Thomas," Anne was saying, "and what works on star-signs or bodily humors you have penned—"

I brought down the earthen jar, pried off the lid, and used a pair of tongs to select the largest and most blood-starved leech.

Chapter

30

HE WAS A GOOD-SIZED BLOOD-SLUG, WITHered from his long fast, glistening and motionless in the lamplight. He looked quite dead. I gave him a slight pinch with the tongs, however, and the sightless creature gave a vigorous twitch.

"Anne, you may wish to enjoy the evening air on deck," I said, with every attempt at sounding sure of myself.

"I will not leave Mother's side," she said. And then, in a lower voice, she added, "You are an accomplished doctor, aren't you, Thomas?"

I could not answer. My desire to be honest with her, and my fears for my patient, created a tangled silence in me.

Anne seemed to realize this. She sighed, and folded her arms, her clothing rustling and casting a shifting shadow across the cabin. But she did not leave.

I set the sleepy leech on the table and used a lancet to prick my finger, an act which in other circumstances would have forced me to brace myself and hesitate. There was no time to ready my will—when blood welled from my finger, I smeared it on the wrist of my patient.

A leech needs a primer—milk or blood—to awaken its appetite to the task. Once placed on this sampling of scarlet, the leech locked onto my patient's flesh. It shrank to a tight, dark orb and then gradually began to swell.

Anne watched all this with an air of anguished approval.

As the leech did its work, I gave Anne a true account of my master's good name, and my own hopes as his assistant. I did not exaggerate my power to cure, but I explained with a truthful heart that no teacher had ever found me the dullest student. I sketched the events of recent days, and she listened.

I had finished my story at last, and she pressed her hands together prayerfully.

Her eyes would not meet mine, and her fingers trembled.

When the leech grew fat, I pried him gently free. A circle of skin where the leech had fed had been removed— only the topmost layer of flesh, as artfully as any a glazier might cut in a church window. I searched among the leeches in the jar for another just as hungry.

"I cannot find Sir Robert," said Hercules, panting and wet with salt spray.

"Maybe he's studying the sky," I suggested. Learned men were always working with star-charts and astrolabes, foretelling future calamities.

"I searched the ship," said Hercules, his voice falling into a song-song recitation of his effort, "among the seamen and the soldiers, and the arms magazine, where gentlemen sometimes like to count the shot and pinch the gunpowder in its sacks. I sought him in among the wine barrels, too, sir, where he might sample the cargo. He is gone."

I considered this. "Hercules, ask the watch on the quarterdeck"—meaning the soldier standing guard there—"to take you to Captain Foxcroft's cabin. I believe Sir Robert must be there."

When fair-haired Hercules had left us again, Anne drew a pomander from a pouch at her belt and took a long breath of healthful spices—their perfume reached me, rose petals and cinnamon. Gentle folk took such fragrance as a bracer, sometimes, when weariness or troubling news put them in need.

To my pleasure and relief she offered me the pomander, a carved boxwood ball with many holes. I breathed the perfume as I heard her say, her voice weak with feeling, "Shipboard physicians are never the best."

"My master was a rare scholar," I protested.

She smiled sadly. "With an even more rare apprentice?"

"I am at your service, Anne."

"I am grateful for your honesty, Thomas Spyre," she said. "You've proven merciful and even wise, and I am grieved at the loss of William Perrivale. But more than anything I fear for my mother's life."

Hercules returned, and barely managed a breathless, "Doctor, Sir Robert is not there either," before Captain Foxcroft's figure loomed behind him, pushing him to one side and stepping into the lamplight of our cabin.

Chapter

3 1

•

THE CAPTAIN INTRODUCED HIMSELF WITH
every courtesy to Anne, and then turned to study my
patient, not before saying, "With your permission, master
surgeon."

My master would have ordered him out of the cabin at
once. I could have done so myself, but the truth is I believed
that the captain had both the rank and experience to over-
ride such insistence from me. Furthermore, I believed that
the captain had the well-being of his crew and his passengers at heart.

And I was more concerned than anyone regarding the
health of my patient. "We have searched the ship," I said.
"We cannot find Sir Robert."

"Perhaps, Thomas," said the captain in an attempt at
wry humor, "Sir Robert has evaporated."

I felt a growing flicker of friendship toward the captain,
a man already visibly worn by his duty to the ship and its
passengers.

There was one cabin Hercules would not have searched.

"Is it possible, my lord captain," I hazarded, "that he is with the admiral?"

Hercules returned at once with Sir Robert.

The distinguished knight and playwright bowed handsomely to Anne, asked the captain to excuse us, and, when we were alone with Anne and her mother, knelt beside my patient.

Sir Robert spoke to me in Latin. When I did not understand what he was saying, he tried an even simpler form of that language. At last I could catch his meaning. "You are right in bleeding her," he said, "but a lancet would be quicker."

"You have my permission," I said, shaping my Latin with care, "to open a vein."

Anne appeared reassured to hear us speaking in the scholar's tongue. She looked on with every show of calm, but I was troubled to hear Sir Robert say, in slowly paced Roman syllables, "I have never cut a blood vessel in my life."

"But you are a man of great learning," I protested, "while I am yet a student." My simple Latin sounded childish in my ears. I added, earnestly, "I am grateful for your help."

"I part with it willingly," said the knight with an expectant smile. "Your hand, I warrant, is far steadier than mine."

I took the lancet in my hand. It was a well-shaped little blade, the sort a lady's servant might use to smear butter on bread—except for its keen edge, whetted fine.

The lancet's shadow approached the pale arm of my patient. I hesitated.

I asked Sir Robert to hold a blanket as a screen, so Anne would not have to see the blade do its work. I had been reluctant to touch Anne's mother with steel, and had hoped that a leech would suffice.

But in the event my hand did not tremble. The blood made a pretty sound, purling from the blue vein in the lady's arm, into the brass basin.

When her mother was breathing easily under a gray wool blanket, her pulse thin but steady, Anne put her hand on my arm.

Her eyes were the umber green of a leaf just touched with autumn.

"I am sorry I questioned you so, Thomas," she said.

I could not bring myself to tell her that she expressed her gratitude all too soon.

Chapter

32

•

THE WEEK THAT FOLLOWED WAS BLESSED.

I forced from my mind both my sorrow, and my fear of the promised warfare. Perhaps I began to believe our voyage would last forever.

The cook finally got his great copper stock pot over a fire in the galley, and we supped on mutton and beef stews, steaming servings of nourishment, with leeks and a new vegetable just then being imported from France, the parsnip. It is a tapered, strong-flavored root, no improvement on the turnip. We dined on what remained of the Plymouth bakers' rye and wheat bread. As a ship's officer I ate at the captain's table now that calm weather could be expected, and I had never eaten better.

I heard no end of seaman's tales, stories of ships punctured by the long, piercing beak of the narwhal, shipwrecked sailors driven by starvation to roast the livers of their departed shipmates. The ship's purser, a round, plumcheeked man named Gilbert Brownsword, in charge of the ship's accounts, winked at me and said that every new officer had to listen to the same purple tales, embellished with each retelling.

The admiral often joined us, and more than once asked me into his cabin afterward for some West Country cider. He convinced me that I had a gilded future sailing for the Queen, and I basked in the hope, strengthened by mutton chops and drink.

And then there was Anne.

Every morning I hurried to see my patient and her daughter. Anne was the one I most wanted to talk to, and she would always open the door to their cabin holding the pomander, offering it to me with a smile, and saying, "It's our worshipful physician, Mother, to pay us a visit."

To keep Mary Woodroofe's lungs clear, I prepared a mixture of spearmint, red fennel, mace, and celery, to be taken nine spoonfuls morning and evening. The medicine should have included the blood of a nine-day-old sow, but none of that was on hand. My patient awakened every morning, sound in spirit, although weak, and with no memory of ever being afraid of me. Indeed, she had no memory of the pirates and their attack at all, a failing not unusual where blows to the head are concerned. Now that her normal humors had returned she proved to be a calm and dignified woman, taking pleasure in her daughter's companionship, and expressing delight whenever Admiral Drake paid them a visit.

"This is the very picture of happiness," she would say, given a cup of spiced wine. Or, after a visit from the admiral, "I am the very picture of pleasure." On greeting me in the morning she would say, "I had the very picture of a good night's sleep."

Her daughter had more variety of expression, noting one morning, "Thomas takes the trouble to comb the snags from his hair, Mother, and to brush the salt off his doublet before he comes to see us. You would think," added Anne, "that he gave a very careful thought to his appearance."

"A young man of quality may well do so," said her mother, taking another sip of wine and cloves.

"As though he were suffering either from vanity," said Anne, making a point of speaking about me as though I were not present, "or the desire to impress someone." Some strong feeling colored her cheeks as she adjusted her mother's blanket and looked sideways in my direction.

"'Pride always overthroweth his master,'" said my patient cheerfully, reciting a well-worn adage.

"I am proud," I rallied, "as every man aboard our ship must be, to have two such ladies as companions."

"Two such ladies," echoed Anne, as though mocking me in some manner that confused my thinking.

We voyaged south through what we called the Great Ocean, the mainland of Europe to the east, the merest shadow, a band of clouds and a hint of land.

We sailed beyond the western outline of France. Jack pointed out features I struggled to be able to see, including the great harbor at Bordeaux, with wine-ships and lighters. As we made way even farther south—off the low, green coast of Portugal—Jack pointed out the river-city of Porto, with its caravels and fisher-boats.

Captain Foxcroft offered me a smile when he took his morning wine on the quarterdeck, and sometimes asked me to join him. From him I learned that the standing rigging of the ship is composed largely of shrouds, the strong ropes attached to the masts and bracing them. The shrouds were laced with transverse ropes up and down their height called *ratlines*—pronounce *rattlins*. The ratlines gave the shrouds their web-like appearance, and afforded mariners a foothold as they clambered to shake out a sail.

The wind was strong, nearly always off the starboard quarter, which Captain Foxcroft said was the prevailing breeze in this ocean, and ideal for sailing. The captain was generous with sea-lore, and despite his steadfast caution, so unlike our admiral's blazing self-confidence, he took pains to inquire that my bereavement was not an undue burden to me.

On rare occasions the *Golden Lion* appeared far behind in our wake, but no other fighting ships kissed the horizon. The soldiers prepared their weapons, and practiced, their halberds crashing as they cross-checked friendly blows.

After hours of practice, I became accustomed to the fume of the wicks and the deafening reports of the guns. Jack gave me a wave through the smoke from time to time, and I waved back. The gunners nodded at me approving-ly—I was the young surgeon who had lost his master, and they extended to me some genial brotherhood, perhaps out of compassion, with a dash of respect.

Each night a seaman hung the usual red stern lamp behind the *Elizabeth Bonaventure,* and in the darkness it was easy to convince ourselves that we were not alone on the sea.

Chapter
33

•

"MY MOTHER AND I WILL BE SAFE, WON'T WE, when the sea battle begins?" Anne asked me one evening when her mother slept.

"What shot could penetrate all these futtocks and ribands?" I responded, parroting some knowledge of the ship's frame I had picked up.

"Thomas, we shall need more armor than simple faith in shipwrights," she responded, putting her hand on mine.

Her touch was warm.

Some heavy-footed commotion somewhere above distracted us momentarily, the captain and the first mate singing out orders, another urgent adjustment to the canvas on the main and mizzen masts.

"I would give my blood and breath to protect you," I said.

Never had I made such an extravagant statement, certainly not to Jane, the doe-eyed landlord's daughter back in London.

"I see, Tom," she said, not the response I had expected.

She gave a warm but pensive smile. "We shall be defended by the good wishes and high hopes of our fighting men."

I could say nothing more, warmed by the hope that she considered me one of the men who would fight.

No doubt a playwright or philosopher could summon the wit to discourse with a lovely woman on a warship. But the noise and cramped quarters, the steps and coughs and heavy tread all around, defeated every hope for intimacy—or even a tender thought. The ship's armorer was busy at his forge, his hammer pealing, the cook was bawling at one of his mates, a laughing, half-serious scolding audible even here, declaiming, "If I had another poxy rabbit-sucker for a mate I'd hang myself."

I stepped closer. It was my sudden intention to kiss her, surprising even myself.

But before I could complete the act, her mother stirred, and coughed.

She sat up, saying, "Anne, the lamp is smoking."

It could not last, this peace.

Gradually the evening came when gunners cleaned their guns, polished them, and sang songs I had not heard before. These were deep-voiced chanteys, with strangely charm-laden lyrics intended not for our ears, but for the benefit of the guns.

Far and true/powder and fire, chants about unerring cannon shots, and an enemy dashed to the Deep.

The whetstones sang on the cutting edges of boarding hooks and daggers, until no greater keenness could be purchased. A quiet came over the deck. Soldiers and mariners put their heads together, callused fingers pointing where a land-haze rose up over the horizon. We rounded some vague shadow-spit of shore.

The admiral uttered the words himself, leaning over the quarterdeck rail as a coastline crept by. "The Spanish mainland," he said. "And a joy to behold."

Wine casks and fishing net drifted on the swells, evidence of Spanish shipping and harbor life. My own heart beat fast, and Jack's eyes met mine with a glow of ill-suppressed excitement.

"Cadiz harbor," murmured Jack, "is less than a day away."

Chapter
34

●

ALL NIGHT WE DID NOT SLEEP, OUR SHIP keeping steady progress under canvas that glowed in the starlight.

Every man whispered now, if he spoke at all. Stories were told of shipboard voices drifting for miles, alerting the enemy. Captain Foxcroft paced, gazing back at the *Golden Lion,* the warship lagging but persistent, growing ever closer.

Admiral Drake was not to be seen for the moment, keeping to his charts and his prayers, we understood, in his cabin. No one was permitted to strike a spark on deck, and soldiers wrapped cloth around their boots to muffle their steps.

Hercules polished my own boots in the shaded lamplight of our cabin, working oil into my sword belt. He had me stand still while he brushed me all over with boar's-hair bristles. I felt like an adventurer.

I asked Hercules if all surgeons went to battle so polished

and darned, and he said, "Of course, sir. There is no other way."

"To do what?" I had to ask.

"To kill," he said simply, "or to die."

On the morning of the seventeenth day we were at sea, the *Elizabeth Bonaventure* came-to, as mariners put it—stopping at a point in the sea swells, and turning into the wind.

The *Golden Lion* drew near, pennons curling and snapping in the breeze out of the northwest, her sails booming and cracking as she made all possible haste to join us. It was a thrill to see this warship, and to observe the sun-brown faces of soldiers and seamen other than our own, the mariners on both vessels too tense with anticipation to wave or call out. A few smaller ships, pinnaces like the one we had sailed out of London, bobbed well behind the *Golden Lion*. There were no additional craft—the refitted merchant warships had been scattered by the weather.

Captain Foxcroft beckoned to me, welcoming me with a care-worn smile as I joined him on the quarterdeck. Sir Robert was there, too, outfitted in high, flared boots, and a broad sword belt with a blazing silver buckle. His features were shaded by the brim of his feathered hat, and, like the captain, he wore a highly polished breastplate.

It was the sight of this armor that quickened my heart and chilled me at the same time. Perhaps I had hoped that some jaunty maneuver would take the place of battle, the capturing of another prize-ship, perhaps, some symbolic defiance while we waited for the bulk of our fleet.

I greeted these men wordlessly, all of us too full of feeling to trust speech. Every creak of the ship's timbers, every hush of sea around her hull, was amplified by my senses. I wondered, too, how many of these sturdy, eager men would be alive to see sunset.

Admiral Drake remained in his cabin.

A lookout called some mariner's warning and men turned to watch a vessel on the horizon. Another vessel loomed in the hint of a harbor not far to the east.

"Spanish fishermen," muttered the captain.

High above, suntanned mariners strained from the castles atop the masts, watching the sea. Men adjusted their swords nervously, and gunners made minute adjustments to the gun carriages. Captain Foxcroft bit his thumbnail, his eyes shifting from point to point on the ocean. We could not tarry here long, right in the sea-road from the mouth of the great enemy harbor of Cadiz.

But with the painstaking slowness I had seen before at sea—keen anticipation offset by agonizing deliberateness—the *Golden Lion,* labored to come even closer. Laces of sea-foam rose and fell around the ships. Vice-Admiral Borough, a wary bear of a man in a brilliantly brocaded jerkin, leaned out over his quarterdeck rail and called some greeting, his words lost in the lift and fall of the sea.

"You led us a merry chase," cried the vice-admiral again, and added some further word.

At that moment the admiral climbed the steps from his cabin.

His breastplate blazed in the full morning sun of the quarterdeck, and the crest of his helmet flashed. His cheeks glowed, and he stood on his tiptoes, gazing around at the ship and her crew, inhaling the salt air.

Every one of us must have been joined by the same eager hope—that Admiral Drake might give us a share of his great confidence.

And that is what he did, taking in the sight of every man under the sky, meeting our gaze with his, and filling each of us with a feeling of promise. He did not forget me, touching my gaze, too.

Admiral Drake gave a nod, studied the wind with a smile of satisfaction, and then turned and spoke quietly to the captain. Captain Foxcroft took a deep, ragged breath. But he obeyed promptly enough, singing out orders in a firm voice.

The ship's trumpeter licked his lips, pursed them experimentally, then lifted his shiny brass horn. A first, thready note was nearly silent. And then the trumpeter tried again, and this time the call lifted, *to arms, to arms.*

Our vessel made for the Spanish harbor, leaving Vice-Admiral Borough bending over the rail of his ship, calling after us in dismay.

Chapter

35

●

APPROACHING THE SPANISH MAINLAND was like watching invisible needles stitching in rocks, castle walls, spires and towers of a city on an illustrated cloth. The wind propelled the vessel forward at a pace that allowed much time to wonder at the hulls and masts growing ever more definite beyond the rocky mouth of the harbor.

Captain Foxcroft kept one hand on the rail of the quarterdeck, and gave the orders Admiral Drake passed on to him. All English flags and pennons, and Drake's own insignia, were struck—brought down—the long, tapered flags fluttering and seeming to struggle against the hands taking them in. False flags were run up, insignia and colors I did not recognize, and the sight of which brought a laugh from Sir Robert.

"They are Flemish flags, if they are anything," he said, in response to my question. The lowland country was in no conflict with any other, and her flag disguised our militant intentions perfectly.

It was afternoon when the sound of sea lapping on rocks

reached us, and that exhalation rose all around of salt and seaweed—the presence of a shore. Which tiny figure along this beach, I wondered, would prove the vigilant sentry who put our lives in danger? A net-mender shaded his eyes. A child stood on a high rock to watch our sails. In the distance, within the mouth of the harbor, fishermen drew in a long net, a boat at the outer circumference of the skein guiding it in.

The captain and admiral made their way down the quarterdeck stairs, and hid below-decks, the admiral barely able to suppress a laugh as he peered out from the shadows. One glimpse of the famous sea fighter *El Draque,* we knew, would be enough to send the port into panic.

But the extreme foolhardiness of our position became all the more clear as we came within range of the harbor defenses.

The entrance to the port of Cadiz was defended by a great stone fortress. A sentry on a low tower watched as our ship made way ever closer. Our warship, followed by her reluctant, laggard companion, could be easily raked and ruined by the fort's archers and cannon.

We inched past the rocky foundation of the citadel. My skin prickled as the distant sentry studied us. He called to a fellow soldier, and soon guards gathered behind the battlements to count our guns. No doubt they wondered why a Flemish warship was in such a hurry to enter Cadiz harbor, a refuge for freighters and their precious cargoes.

In their armor and halberds, these Spaniards looked more colorful than their English counterparts, more fond of canary yellow sleeves. Their beards were uniformly dark, their teeth bright as they pointed out our guns, merely curious, it seemed, what our mission might be. Ross Bagot, our master gunner, making every show of innocent lounging, lifted a languid hand in greeting to the Spanish guards.

My friend Jack and a wiry gunner's mate named Chubbs manned one of the smaller weapons that projected out over the main deck. Jack's gun was angled so it would fire at any vessel approaching off the starboard bow, should one appear. Jack, too, made a dumb-show of innocent activity, prompted by the master gunner to a theatrical preoccupation with a flaw in a leather bucket. The ship's mates passed among the seamen, encouraging a show of harmless knotting and scrubbing.

Flemish or not, our vessel kindled the curiosity of the sentries. A Spanish soldier hefted a musket. I could see him judge the aim and range, with no real intention of discharging the firearm. He was already losing the opportunity as our ship took on greater momentum, the wind muscling her forward, white water parting wide at our prow.

The *Golden Lion* followed, and the few pinnaces in her wake. They met with no more hostility than we had encountered, the soldiers at last relaxing and retiring behind the battlements.

"It's as easy as kiss-the-duchess," I said hopefully—it had been one of my master's favorite phrases.

"The king of Spain," observed Sir Robert, "has all his cannon pointed toward land. No one here expects an attack from the sea."

The captain and the admiral were back on the quarterdeck, the admiral indicating the array of ships that lay ahead, merchantmen and caravels, lighters and fishing boats, too many ships to fit along the wharves, many of the great hulls anchored off shore. Gilded wine-ships, multi-colored galleons—some of the vessels were surely loaded with silks, or even silver ingots and bricks of pure gold.

The admiral motioned for me to join him, and I was surprised that my knees were steady despite my pounding pulse. Now that we had stolen past the fortress I began to allow myself a hopeful lightening of spirits. Perhaps warfare would now prove just another sport, the taking of a rich cargo or two, and a speedy escape.

A horseman left the stone fort, looking our way from time to time as he rode with increasing purpose back into town, a cloak flowing out behind as the steed rocked into a gallop.

We were in the harbor now, with no easy way of turning back. Many of us counted the ships before us and around us, warships and galleys among them. Mouths worked silently, fingers ticking off the magnificent ships anchored in the peaceful waters.

Sixty vessels.

Our crew was quiet, and I tried hard to disguise my fear.

Chapter
36

TROUBLE DID NOT TAKE LONG IN SEEKING us out.

A bank of oars flashed in the late afternoon sun.

A galley separated from the tangle of merchant ships, and sped toward us. She was followed by another very like it in appearance, trim, sleek, oar-powered vessels able to race easily against the wind. They skimmed the water in a breathtaking show of swiftness, maneuvering deftly around a stout merchant ship anchored in the middle of the harbor.

The nearby merchant freighter had caught the admiral's eye. "She's an argosy," Drake said—a rich merchantman. "Look at her stern, painted scarlet and blue," he laughed. "And the gilded frames around her gunports. She's Genoese, Sam, and heavy in the water with something rich!" The Genoans were world renowned as among the most successful sea traders.

It was the first time I had heard the admiral use the captain's Christian name, and Captain Foxcroft gave an appreciative if strained smile, humoring his ambitious admiral. "She'll have us in range soon," said the captain, running a calculating eye over the handsome Italian ship. "By my count, she's carrying forty guns."

"She'll need every one of them," said Admiral Drake.

Immediately our attention was distracted by the rapidly approaching galleys, as quick and silent as two driving water-snakes, their wakes cutting wide of the treasure ship. Their white oars gleamed, the skilled oarsmen making easy work of halving the distance to us, and halving it again.

Guns gleamed in the prow of the foremost galley, twin cannon being primed as we looked on. The bronze guns were on swivels, meaning that they could be aimed with accuracy. Armed men gathered amidships, official-looking in their dark armor and slashed silk sleeves. Sir Robert rested his hand easily on the hilt of his rapier, and I made every effort to look as carefree.

The galley began to back oars, slowing her darting approach. The swivel guns were elevated and swung from side to side, the gunners letting us take in the implication of their choice of targets—first the mainmast, then the mizzen, and then the cluster of officers on our quarterdeck.

Our own gunners shielded the fuming wicks in their hands, our soldiers swarming below-decks.

A galley officer, with a shining breastplate and scarlet-slashed sleeves, stepped to the rail of his ship. The speaking trumpet in his hand gleamed.

The port official's voice was clear in the calm late afternoon, his words projected by the implement in his hand, and made all the clearer by the continuing, slowing approach of the galley. He called to us in a tongue I could not name—Flemish, perhaps. And then in French, a language I had heard in the London streets.

Captain Foxcroft made every effort to act the harmless visiting sea captain, eager to understand but not quite able to comprehend the query, one hand to his ear. The exchange was normal and proper so far—royal customs men were seeking to verify the origin and intent of an arriving vessel. It was not the first time that day that I wondered at the handsomeness and peaceful dignity of the Spaniards, well appointed in clothing and in arms, expecting to carry out their duties without violence.

One of the darkly bearded officers must have seen something that alarmed him. He stepped briskly to the side of the port official.

Whatever was murmured into his ear froze the officer at the rail, speaking trumpet halfway to his lips.

Admiral Drake could not disguise his red beard and blue eyes any longer. The famous sea fighter gave an order. A single pennon was run up along the mast, snapping straight in the wind—Drake's personal insignia, the dragon with its sharpened talon claiming the round world.

The admiral spoke again, his voice quiet and steady. The captain raised a hand, like someone greeting a friend. Ross Bagot, the master gunner, standing in the ship's waist—the main deck directly before the quarterdeck— turned to his mates and his lips moved, calling out the command relayed to the gunners below.

I never caught the words.

Sooner than the thought can be formed our starboard gun-ports were opened all along the gun deck below with a sur-prising clatter. The cannons ran out, carriage wheels squealing.

Then a few heartbeats of silence were broken by commotion from the galley, excited Spanish commands, oars thrashing the water.

I wished I could hang on to a rail, or hurry forward and fling my arms around the mainmast. Fear kept me where I was, alive to what was about to happen. I wanted only to stop the great wheel of days, and reverse every hour.

Our guns fired, and the ship shuddered under my feet.

Chapter

37

●

THE SMOKE BURNED MY EYES.

It was too thick to breathe, a thick atmosphere of yellow and black fumes. As the breeze dispersed the clouds, the wreckage on the galley deck was clear, the mess that had been officers and men strewn across the deck. The galley's swivel guns fired just then, but with no apparent damage to our ship as soldiers swarmed out from our hold, English fighting men taking their positions.

Harquebusses were aimed and discharged, and archers climbed into our top castles. Soon arrows crisscrossed the deck of the galley. The galley resembled an insect stunned and unable to command her many limbs. Then her oars dug into the water, and the galley began a slow turn.

Her men loosed every variety of weapon at us, harque-bus fire clawing the air, pistol shots adding their smoke to the general obscurity, arrows and even leaden slingshot rattling across our deck. Spanish officers shielded wounded men with their bodies. I could not suppress a feeling of sharp compassion for these warriors, and I was aware of the stark unfairness of our sudden attack.

The galley's stern guns came into play, shot from the two cannons howling high overhead, missing us entirely and skipping out across the water beyond. The oared vessel retreated, bits of timber strewn across the water. Her sister ship joined her in speedy flight, and our gunners cheered, their chorus of voices thin after the din of gunfire.

But we had barely begun.

An entire fleet of oared warships darted forward through the water. The retreating, battered galleys forced their way through this deploying fleet, some ten sleek man-powered vessels. The *Golden Lion* maneuvered, turning her starboard guns in the direction of the advancing Spaniards, and despite my misgivings the sight made me proud—an English ship spewing fire, her shot skipping across the water.

Our own gunners, too, splashed shot among the galleys, and a well-aimed round shattered a row of oars. The galleys tangled with one another, rowing implements angled use-lessly in the air. At last they managed to turn about and race back toward the shelter of the wharf, as our men cheered once again.

The Genoese ship had weighed her anchor, seamen tiny at this distance scurrying about her deck, clambering upward and shaking out her great white sails.

Our ship closed on her, the big merchant ship low in the water and slow to respond to her rudder. As the handsome vessel opened her gunports, other merchant vessels were in plain view beyond, in the waters near the wharf. It seemed to me that this cargo ship was not laboring to escape, after all, but working deliberately to bring her guns to bear.

"She's too heavy to flee," Admiral Drake remarked to me. "And she's got some spleen in her—she's going to make a fight of it."

"She's protecting her fellow merchantmen," I suggested.

"How very brave of her," said Drake with a brisk smile. He turned to Captain Foxcroft. "Give her some shot in the belly, Sam," he said, in the tone of a man deciding a cheerful wager, "but be careful our gunners don't sink her."

It seemed like days ago that our shipmates had been tidy-looking mariners, pretending to be harmless and lazy, fresh-faced and calm. Now they were sweaty devils, grinning with enthusiasm as cannon thrust forward through the ports, aimed, and answered the command to fire with another deafening broadside.

The Genoese returned the fire, salt spray dousing the quarterdeck. Our ship maneuvered closer, the Genoese mariners no longer small, scrambling figures but broad-shouldered men, ramming charges down the throats of their maindeck guns.

This time one of the enemy shots struck our ship, a resounding blow that shook the rigging. The admiral gave a glance upward. Warships like ours were famous for their stout timbers, but the gaunt expression on our captain's face told me that another volley or two would begin to cripple our vessel.

Color in his cheeks, the admiral gave the order, "Pay them back in kind, Captain Foxcroft."

The battle that followed could have taken a few minutes or it could have consumed many hours. The sun, which had been retiring toward the sea behind us, stopped in its descent, and the wind ceased, our sails and the canvas of our enemy hanging slack.

The Genoese gunports spouted fire, and our own gunners vanished in the poisonous, lung-searing smoke. At times there was silence, except for the gasping of the gunners, swabbing the gun barrels, jamming home a charge of powder, working round lead shot down the muzzles of our cannon.

Then, once again, the near-silence was obliterated by the thunder of gunfire.

When the smoke lifted from time to time, the Genoese treasure ship was stripped of rigging, ropes dangling, scraps of clothing and flesh sown across her maindeck. Her gunwales gaped, and bloody men wrestled a gun back into its port. Pistol shots whipped our deck from her fighting tops—the firing positions high on the masts—answered by muskets and longbows of our own.

It took so long to reload a firearm or a cannon, so many deliberate well-rehearsed steps, that for long moments the fight seemed to take place underwater, mates slowly reaching for their powder scoops, gunners bending down to use their bronze reamers, singed fingers cradling another round shot, all performed with a sodden rhythm.

Everything else we had ever accomplished in our lives was far off and colorless, now. We could barely remember any other place but this calm, suddenly windless late day. Our ship rocked with yet another broadside.

I had heard of ships weakened and sunk during battle without suffering an enemy blow, planks and pegs loosened by the recoil of their own guns. The Genoese ship was holed now, three ragged shot-wounds near the waterline.

And more damage was exposed as the water lifted and fell away, an ugly stitching of bright wounds along her hull. As she let loose another uneven broadside the recoil rocked the treasure ship gently back, and predictably forward again. Each time this happened the ragged punctures in her hull dipped downward, into the brine.

At last water began to flow through her gunports and then up, over her gunwales, tide stretching across her deck.

Chapter
38

"BOARD HER BEFORE SHE SINKS!" CRIED
Drake.

But as our stern swung slowly toward the freighter, the
merchant guns continued to bark fire at us, and men in our
ship's waist ducked involuntarily as some new variety of
shot shrilled through the air, an ugly, stomach-turning
sound.

"It's chain shot," remarked the admiral to me. "Meant
to cut our men to pieces."

The big cargo ship was burning now, the lapping, rising
harbor water kissing flames, white steam lifting. Gun
smoke mixed with the reek of burning cargo, some distinc-
tive odor the admiral recognized. "Raw silk!" cried
Admiral Drake in anguish, striking the rail with his fist.
"Tons of the stuff."

At last the ship sank. There was nothing to be done.
The battle-hewed cargo ship went down, a swirl of water
over her masts, and the fume of smoke lingering, slowly

spinning, over the tangle of cordage and splinters that belched up out of the water.

I had heard of such disasters, but had always imagined survivors, clinging to spars and drift-planks, men swimming to assist their shipmates. Plenty of useless wreckage burst to the surface, and a single, floating human arm, but no human struggle, triumphant or otherwise, played out across the water. Our nearness to such great loss of life, scores of men drowning while we stood, gave me a pang of nausea.

"This is a grievous waste," said Drake. "And yet—as our Lord Jesus decides." He turned to me with a smile. "We'll get our hands on treasure yet."

Night fell.

Anne and her mother were safe in their cabin, the door fastened shut. Anne would open it only after questioning me, saying she did not believe I was Thomas Spyre—the young man she had known would not have participated in such a thunderous battle.

"It's me, in truth," I insisted earnestly. "Wanting only to see you."

Anne held the pistol as she opened the door. "I keep it primed and bent," she said, answering the question I had not brought myself to ask.

Loaded and cocked, she meant. "There's little danger to you and your mother," I said. The ringing in my ears made me unsure whether I spoke too loudly, or too softly. Mariners who had been to war were often half deaf for the rest of their lives.

"You speak of danger," said Anne, her eyes friendly even as her tone was cool. "You stood on deck, as I imagine, with timber fragments cutting off heads all around."

"I believe heads remained attached to bodies," I responded. "On our ship."

Her mother was sitting up in her bunk, a blanket drawn up to her chin. Her eyes were bright with fear, and I put a hand to her forehead. It was cool. I had feared that the percussive force of so much gunfire might have done her harm.

She spoke so quietly I could barely hear her. I thought I made out the words, "I am the picture of terror."

"When is Admiral Drake," Anne demanded, "going to turn this ship about and back to sea?"

"He does not confide his every thought to me," I responded. I was trying to make light of the matter, but I sounded—I realized too late—dismissive.

"Is our admiral mad?" Anne asked. "Has he shared his madness with his officers and his crew like a kind of plague?"

Words fled me.

"Is there no peace-loving man," asked Anne, "aboard this ship?"

"I have a remembrance for you," I said, a little speech I had memorized. "And I pray that it might bring you luck."

Only as I extended my gift to her did I realize how inappropriate it looked—a twisted, claw-like relic.

She put her hands behind her involuntarily. She gave me a courteous smile, but her eyes said *What is it?*

"The fighting spur of Pepper John," I said, feeling every bit the coarse, ill-spoken knave. What had inspired me, I asked myself, to offer her such an ugly gift? I heard my voice continue, "The bird was a legend among fighting cocks."

"The foot of a warrior chicken," replied Anne.

"A humble offering," I said, my voice clouded with shame.

She accepted it, cupping her hand around it gingerly. "A token of your regard?" she asked.

"Of that, and my good wishes," I managed.

"Your very good wishes?"

"Indeed, perhaps even my love."

Had I said too much?

"I shall keep it among my treasures, Tom," she said. And she added, perhaps to banish the doubt in my eyes, "Truly I will."

She did something then that made me marvel long afterward.

She put her lips on mine.

I was more pleased to see Hercules than I would have imagined, especially to see him unhurt. He was in the surgeon's cabin, where he had set out an array of medical implements on our table, as I had instructed. As surgeon's mate he had to stand duty here, receiving patients or attending them. Hercules peered around the cabin doorway, and did not seem eager to step beyond its threshold.

"No reports of anyone splinter-torn," he announced. "Or shot-ripped, sir, or anything of the kind."

His eyes were full of questions. I knew he wanted me to tell what I had seen on the quarterdeck while he stood watch here, protected but confined. I peered into the jar of leeches, and felt a protective urge even toward those dumb creatures. I shook the jar, and they each gave a sullen, sleepy twitch.

"Hercules," I consoled him, astonishing myself with my own careless tone, "you missed no great sight."

I performed my duty as surgeon, moving about the ship, greeting soldiers and seamen, and hearing from all hands that there were no injuries. A few gunners had blisters from setting their hands on hot gun barrels, but these were not considered wounds, and my queries of concern were met with laughing. "It's just a kiss, doctor, and nothing to be worried about." Or words to that effect—the accents and phrases were sometimes unfamiliar, but the voices determined and full of good cheer.

The ship's crew and fighting men were excited, but it was another kind of joy than the peaceful anticipation we had experienced on the open sea.

The tide was ebbing—the one that would have carried us to safety if Drake had decided to escape. Apparently, he had decided to spend the night here. Our ship, and the *Golden Lion* and a few other modest English vessels, were surrounded in the darkness of the enemy harbor.

We were trapped.

Chapter
39

•

VICE-ADMIRAL BOROUGH WAS ON HIS WAY
toward our ship, his boat rowed by a crew across the short
interval between the two warships, the oars making rhythmic splashes in the water.

The night was cold, and dark enough to make me wish
for the all-seeing eyes of an owl. But some of the late-arriving
English pinnaces had sacked a small merchant ship, abandoned by its terrified crew, and set the vessel alight. Flames
from the ship climbed the masts and illuminated the black
harbor.

The port of Cadiz itself was a source of light. Barrels of
pitch burned in well-spaced rows along the wharf, and the
outline of the monuments and churches of the town were
pricked out by lamps and torch lights.

Church bells had been sounding an alarm, and halberds
and lances gleamed where soldiers were mustering in the
town squares. Guns rumbled, hauled unseen by horses, and
Jack had whispered to me that a new battery was being

prepared, on a slope overlooking the harbor.

Admiral Drake and Captain Foxcroft greeted the vice-admiral with every courtesy, and I stood with the purser, Gilbert Brownsword, and other worthies of the ship, Sir Robert, Ross Bagot, and various master sergeants among them.

Vice-Admiral Borough was a solidly set man with a square head and the stumpy, strong legs of many seasoned mariners. He had thinning brown hair and a stylishly short beard. He ran his eyes over the company assembled to welcome him on the quarterdeck, and as Drake introduced me, Vice-Admiral Borough remarked, "Verily, Admiral, your surgeon's a youth."

"Let him lance a vein, and you'll be young again, too," said Drake with a laugh, and I was grateful for the smile the famous knight gave me, before he descended the stairs with the vice-admiral.

The two secluded themselves in Drake's cabin. Captain Foxcroft breathed on his hands, and when he caught my eye he approached me and murmured, in a low voice, "I pray the vice-admiral will persuade our worthy leader to preserve our lives."

I was stirred by this frank concern on the part of our captain. "Do you think the danger very great?" I found myself asking.

The captain gave a humorless laugh. "It could not be greater."

Officers from the two ships mingled on our quarterdeck, huddled in wool mantles against the night chill while all around us, across the water, came the sounds of hooves and military-sounding commands, a town ready for battle.

Vice-Admiral Borough stumped up to the quarterdeck to gaze across the black water, toward the vague outline of his own ship.

Captain Foxcroft joined him, and I heard Vice-Admiral Borough say, "Drake believes he will make them spend the best blood in their bellies."

The captain inclined his head thoughtfully. "By which he means—?"

"He means to burn every ship in the port," said the vice-admiral, "sift them of every gold *real,* and if he could sail across bare land the many miles to King Philip's bedchamber in the Escorial he would do it." He shook his head in silent exasperation.

Captain Foxcroft slumped at this confirmation, leaning against the quarterdeck rail, but the other officers straightened, hands finding sword hilts, chins lifting. Even I, sharing our captain's doubt, felt a thrill.

And more than a little uneasiness.

When the vice-admiral had been rowed back to his own ship Drake gave the command to make way farther into the inner harbor.

In the glimmering illumination of far-off pitch lamps, seamen leaped eagerly to their duties. Our warship eased forward, the bare wind and slack tide just enough to propel us among the widely dispersed cargo ships.

We had selected a large, dark profile—a freighter lower in the water that our own, and showing not a single light. As we approached this vessel she came alive. Weapons glinted, men gathering on her maindeck.

"Can you fight two-handed?" asked the admiral, suddenly at my side.

I answered that I could.

It was true—I had studied the technique of fighting with a knife in my left hand, and the rapier in my right. Drake pressed a dagger into my hand, a short stout blade with a leather-wrapped grip.

"I took it from a Spanish captain," said the admiral, "in the days when I robbed gold fresh from the mines." It was a matter of legend, Drake intercepting the mule trains in the jungle mountains of the New World, scattering the armed guards. "It's my gift to you, Thomas," he added, "in the Queen's name."

I could barely find words to express my thanks.

"I want you to board with the fighting men," said the admiral.

I tucked the dagger into my sword belt, taking deep breaths, as I had been trained, preparing myself for swordplay.

"Stay near Sir Robert," said Admiral Drake. "Do everything you can to keep him alive."

"Indeed, my Lord Admiral," I said earnestly, "everything in my power."

"He might pen a play about me some day—if his muse is equal to the task."

"No doubt you'll inspire many a poet," I returned, happy to delay my departure in conversation.

The admiral laughed and squared the cloak on my shoulders. "And take care to preserve yourself, too, while you're about it."

Chapter

40

•

I FOLLOWED THE ATTACKING, CLATTERING tumult of armed humanity, leaping down into the cargo ship.

For much of the night's fighting I had known that we were striking an enemy as well as seeking treasure, crippling the ships that would otherwise raid our homeland. That defensive necessity was a spur to our fighting. But now I began to sense battle-gluttony among my fellows, a fierce joy in doing harm. I sensed it in the hoarse voices of my fellow fighters, and it made me feel unclean.

The rapier was in my fist, but pressed against my leg by the crush of fighting men around me. I could not have slipped and fallen even if I had stumbled badly—I was held upright by the press of bodies yelling and struggling forward across the deck.

If anything, Sir Robert kept my own head from being split, fighting well with his blade, skewering an arm brandishing an ax, kicking, bellowing threats, and lashing yet another attacker across the face. Enemy seamen began to abandon the vessel, dropping down into boats on the far side of the ship. The purser's mates called up from the cargo hold, "She's full of iron, sir, great black pig-bricks of it."

Gilbert Brownsword half stumbled, half lowered himself down into the hold, the dark, metallic tang of iron in the air, rust-sour. He was up again soon, calling out toward our quarterdeck, "Crude iron, my lord," and Drake's command rang from the flagship, "Burn her to the waterline."

Some twenty ships were set alight by our fighting men, as they searched for coin and treasures, carrying off gilded statues and silver flagons, plated candlesticks and weapons, destroying what they could not easily carry, or was not worth the effort—like a load of iron. Sometimes a ship's crew would set a vessel burning as we boarded, out of spite, or to prevent us from stealing her contents.

I attended a few bruises, helped a stunned soldier or two climb to his feet, but there were virtually no injuries to the forces from our ship, and as a surgeon I found little demand for my fledgling prowess.

I stayed with Sir Robert all through the darkest hours of the night, boarding one ship after another, and while we often had our weapons drawn, we did little further fighting. It seemed to me that such rapine demanded a violent sort of greed, but caused little injury, boarding axes and crowbars the most important weapons.

This remained true until we boarded the last, great hulk of a vessel.

She was so close to the wharf that the decks were brightly illuminated by the burning barrels of pitch along the shore. We could hear the curses and taunts of soldiers in the *Corregidor,* the tall stone citadel in town.

We sprang upon this ship like men who had never labored at any other occupation, none of us stumbling, now, every man an expert. But at once this was not like the other vessels we had sacked. The men here were determined, perhaps because the citizens of the town were spectators, nearby and in danger from us, and our own fighting men were growing both over-confident and tired.

Spanish pikemen battled our soldiers, backed by officers with drawn rapiers. Halberds and Welsh-hooks clattered against the staves of Spanish pikes. Our soldiers made progress, foot-to-foot against the defenders, but then the wall of defenders began to push us back. We locked arms with them, a living tangle of sweating creatures. A wooden weapon snapped, a Spanish helmet clattered and broke, struck by the iron bill of a weapon, but the mass of wrenching, grunting men were knotted, neither side strong enough to win.

I struggled through this tangle of fighting folk, and found Sir Robert, engaging a gentleman swordsman at one end of the struggling mass. "Dog-livered knave, I'll make you sweat," Sir Robert cried, with a playwright's zest.

I wondered if he had rehearsed this remark privately— it did not sound like an inspiration of the moment. I felt yet another instant of great fondness and protectiveness for this gentleman of so many talents.

But perhaps Sir Robert was also weary from his long

night's labor. He fought well enough at first against this Spaniard. The man was built like a wine barrel on two legs, a stout, thick-legged gentleman in a plumed hat—a thick-necked, heavy-shouldered sword-fighter. Their rapiers glinted in the sudden spill of light from a pitch barrel knocked over on the quarterdeck, and as this flame erupted even higher the eyes of the two combatants took on a scarlet, flickering glow.

But as the fight ensued it was plain that Sir Robert was too tired. He did not embarrass himself with his stance, holding his blade in the flexible grip of a skilled fighter. But he was only just escaping being cut to the quick, his opponent's blade much faster, and wielded by a more muscular and far less weary arm.

I called out, trying to distract the Spaniard, but in my own fatigue I had no more voice than a housefly. Sir Robert and the Spaniard clinched, the larger man trying to wrestle the Englishman off his feet, gouging at Sir Robert's eyes with his gloved hand.

Blood suddenly gleamed underfoot, flowing from the tangle of soldiers, the result of some pikeman's injury. Sir Robert slipped, one arm wheeling. He kept his footing, but then he slipped once more.

And fell.

He struck the deck hard.

The Spaniard proceeded to kick Sir Robert, his heavy boot striking the knight in the chest.

I cut at the Spaniard with my sword, trying to drive him

back, but merely sliced the air. I drew my dagger, and began to pull together what tactics I could remember of two-handed fighting.

The Spanish officer smiled at me, and uttered a crisp, foreign challenge. He added a further taunt, a string of syllables I could not understand.

I was quick, and, under the circumstances, fairly accurate. My teacher would have approved as my blade punctured my enemy's cloak, and tore into his doublet. The budding surgeon in me sensed the long, flexible blade enter my opponent's skin, run along the meat and gristle of his rib cage, and thrust out through the cloak on his back.

The Spaniard's sword dropped, but he gave no sign of falling dead—it was a far from mortal wound. He struck me hard on the chin with the heel of his hand, jarring me loose from the handle of my weapon. He seized the blade near the hilt with his gloved hand, and withdrew it from his flesh, an act of considerable will. Then he flung my rapier across the bloody deck and closed with me, seizing me like a wrestler.

He grappled with me, gouging at my eyes with one hand, throttling me with the other. The dagger in my left hand ripped into the wool of his cloak, unable to cut into him because of the thick fabric. Breath sawed in and out of us, and we danced, wrestling, supporting each other even as we labored to get a killing grip on each other's throats.

He groaned involuntarily, the rapier wound beginning to cause him pain, and I released him. It was a surprise to me, but the logic was clear nonetheless. He was hurt, and I was accustomed to bandaging wounds, and reassuring the injured, not in causing further agony.

"Yield, sir," I heard myself say in a ragged voice. I pressed the point of my dagger to his cheek, the fine steel alive in the fire light.

Chapter
41

HELMETED SOLDIERS BROKE UP OUR COMBAT, a Welsh-hook thrust with little art into my opponent's face.

The heavy iron missed him, but the shaft of the weapon bruised me, a second soldier thrusting toward the Spaniard's belly, and likewise missing.

The Spanish gentleman fell back, blood streaming down the shank of his boots, and offered me some remark in his beautiful, incomprehensible tongue. I was struck by reluctant admiration for this plumed gentleman. He was courteous and well spoken, in contrast to the hard-breathing English soldiers at my side, threatening him with fatigue in their voices, their street-worn language, *poxy, whoreson, Papist,* all they could think of in the face of what sounded like proud poetry.

The Spaniard vanished, fleeing into the afterdeck of the vessel as I retrieved my sword from the shadows.

The big cargo ship was alight, now, flames leaping as our ship shoved off, our seamen doing everything they could to keep the fire from spreading to our vessel.

Soldiers stretched Sir Robert out on the deck of the *Elizabeth Bonaventure.*

The English knight did not move. He did not respond to me when I spoke, or when I rubbed his hands.

"Is he hurt badly, Tom?" was the admiral's question, as he looked down from the quarterdeck.

"My Lord Admiral," I said, "he is for the moment insensible."

I sent Hercules for a long hollow goose quill and a pouch of ground black pepper, recalling the many times I had seen bears awakened by their handlers from near death.

I blew several grains of pepper into Sir Robert's right nostril.

The knight opened his eyes and shut his mouth. He put out a hand, and sat up, readying and yet further readying a massive sneeze that would not come. I prayed that a great convulsion would not do him harm—cracked ribs can gouge a lung as well as any knife.

And when it did come at last, a thunderous blast, he fell back again, blinking and looking around at the masts and rigging above.

"You are well, Sir Robert," I said, half assertion, half hopeful question.

With Sir Robert drowsy in his berth, dosed with aqua vitae and swearing that the pain was an easy burden, I felt the loss of his companionship. And I realized more fully how I had come to anticipate his advice.

"Stay at his side," I cautioned Hercules. "And if he spits blood—"

"Sir, if he swoons or pukes I'll seek you out," said Hercules in his eager sing-song. He added, in a tone of genuine concern for my feelings, "Sir, he will not die."

"How can you be sure, lad?" asked Sir Robert in a tone of sleepy good humor, eavesdropping from his bed.

"If you please, sirs," replied Hercules, "aboard a ship, a cracked rib is more common than a bruise."

I answered a summons to the quarterdeck.

I found Anne there, the admiral pointing across the dark harbor, showing off the blazing skeletons of ships all around.

"Sir Robert's friendship warms me more than his art," said the admiral, when I had given him a brief report on the scholar's condition. "But he's the very man to write a book of this voyage. 'The King of Spain Bearded, Stripped of His Fleet and Mocked.' Or some such."

Drake left us suddenly, and with no further word, called away by some commotion in the forward part of the ship. Captain Foxcroft was calling out frenzied commands, his voice hoarse with the strain of this long night.

"Mother is tart and well armed," said Anne, "with the pistol in her lap."

"She'll blast away the life of any man who peeks in at her," I protested.

"Then you'd best remain here on the quarterdeck," said Anne, "and watch the dawn."

There was indeed a strange peacefulness just then. The air, poisoned by the fumes from burning cargoes, tar-cured rigging and spruce-wood masts, was sweetened by a fresh wind. The perfume of a land breeze swept the quarterdeck for an instant, citrus, red wine and fertile fields. The stars in the east were just beginning to vanish.

"You are too much the physician," said Anne with a sideways glance at me. "Not every limb is waiting to be torn from its body, master surgeon."

"Perhaps not," I admitted.

"Besides," she said, leaning toward me confidingly, "the pistol in my mother's lap has never been loaded with shot."

"Never?"

"Before God, Tom, all along I had powder, but no shot."

I absorbed this news with an incredulous laugh.

"Not that it was harmless when you discovered us," she continued. "I'd rammed in enough gunpowder to spit fire a yard long."

I was about to respond to this, when the commotion at the ship's prow grew louder, and I hurried to the quarter-deck rail to see what was wrong.

A vessel rose toward us on the incoming tide.

A giant thing, she was a source of light as flames fluttered upward from her deck, igniting her rigging, the harbor water around her gilded and scarlet. Her sail filled with the breeze, one span of canvas blushing as the flames lapped at the yard arm. As we watched, the canvas ignited, the ship ablaze along her full length.

"A fire-ship!" cried a frightened voice.

The blazing monster breasted the water, compelled by wind and tide in our direction. I tried to tell myself that she would miss us, certainly.

But heartbeat followed heartbeat, and she swelled larger than ever, and closer. The *Elizabeth Bonaventure* would not respond to her rudder, cornered in the harbor by the sudden sea breeze.

Chapter
42

•

THE WIND PLAYED THROUGH THE FIRE-
ship, sending ember-flags and scraps of flame.

I shielded Anne from a rain of sparks as a living, clawing
ember the size of a man's hand spun down upon us. I dashed
it to dead ash in an instant, but the roar of the flames was
too loud for us to hear each other now. The air was dragged
upward toward the monster as she bore down on us.

She was an old-fashioned ship, with both a towering
forecastle, and a similar fighting structure in the stern.
Years of tar and fiber hammered into fissures in her planks,
spilled pitch and decades of stored victuals, no doubt olive
oil and bacon fat, all erupted out of her timbers now. Her
sailcloth bellied as heat made us cringe, our crew and fighting men crouching, some of them falling to the deck as the
withering heat and noon-day brightness of her blaze
approached.

Anne was calling something to me, but I could not hear
her. It was impossible to breathe, the air robbed from our
lungs.

"Go get your mother!" I cried, my words snatched from my lips by the thunderous updraft. If we had to abandon our ship, Mary Woodroofe would need help.

Anne left me to grope her way to the quarterdeck rail and accepted a bucket from the hands of a seaman. She emptied water over a spray of embers. Amidships men were pouring urine from the piss-barrels over the steaming coals raining down through the rigging.

Captain Foxcroft called out orders that could not be heard. A score of men were bravely poised with boarding hooks, long implements used in securing one ship to another, and at times like these, in warding off an approaching threat. But the heat was too great as the fire storm grew ever nearer, and the men wilted.

Admiral Drake waved to me, with the desperate but spirited manner of a man greeting a long-abandoned friend through a snowstorm. I hurried to him, half falling through the tempest.

The admiral hefted one end of a long, stout oar in my hand, one of the sweeps ships use in rowing against river currents. He called out some fierce encouragement, but I was deaf to every sound but the upward avalanche of the heat.

Jack Flagg and Ross Bagot seized another sweep, and the four of us made way toward the prow of our vessel.

There was a majesty to this mountain of fire as she came on, a ruined, cavernous three-master, her rigging dancing with flame.

We met the seething beakhead of her prow with the

extended ends of our sweeps. The heat fried the ends of my hair, a tickling, sickening sensation all over my scalp, and every breath was a bite of emptiness, all air gone. The momentum of the huge vessel rocked us back, but other men joined us, getting a hand hold on the long oars, others pushing with pikes and staves, all of us leaning into the roiling hulk.

Chapter

43

●

UNTIL THEN, IN MY FOOLISHNESS, I BELIEVED
that I had some degree of courage.

And some enduring confidence. I was certain that we
would not be destroyed by her, even as the burning vessel
passed by, pushed along by our efforts with the sweeps, her
yard arms tumbling into the harbor. Even when a ship's boy
emptied a bucket of salt water over me—"Your doublet is
smoking, sir!"—I did not allow myself to acknowledge
what I felt. We were desperate, but somehow I was nearly
convinced that it was all play-acting, a childish shoving
match in a sudden drizzle of fire.

Only when she was past us, parting water inexorably
toward the wharf with its docked ships, did I understand
how frightened I had been.

I was weak with relief.

Anne embraced me all too briefly, and hurried below-
decks to be with her mother.

The sun was rising, and the Spanish ships against the

wharf were alive with men, struggling up and down the rigging, a panic in each vessel. The receding fire-ship nosed in among them, her castles falling in, sending cascades of sparks upward into the fading stars.

Mariners pressed around me for burn medicine, and I pasted my master's recipe—tallow mixed with pulped turnips—on hands and arms, cheeks and shins, harmless but painful blisters. I smeared injuries with this healing butter, until the crock was half empty. I smeared some of the preparation on my own face, and on my forearms.

Drake put a cup of cider into my grasp, leaning against the quarterdeck rail. His features were smudged, his breastplate freckled with ash, but he raised his cup and toasted the Queen with a smile, like a commander at the beginning of a campaign, not a leader after a long night of battle. I have never tasted more delicious drink.

"Young master surgeon," asked the admiral, "what do you think of our little harbor skirmish?"

I surveyed the smoking wrecks, strewn across the sunrise-silver waters of the harbor. The town was obscured by this haze, and as the fire-ship guttered, burned down to her waterline, I could not keep my heart from feeling a pang of compassion for the many mariners who would be without a ship on this chilly, bitter morning. There was a stirring of humanity, too, boats arriving to salvage the smoking ruins, and the ominous glint of muskets as platoons of foot soldiers hurried along the shore.

My heart sank at the sight—we would not escape unpunished.

"I think Her Majesty will be pleased with our Lord Admiral," I offered, remembering my best manners. My voice was that of a stranger, old and without strength.

"But she will wonder why we sank and burned more than we sacked," said Drake with a wistful shake of his head. "Even though we have plucked and roasted many ships that would have sailed against her kingdom."

When admiralty officials heard my report in London, I would have to answer honestly. If the famous knight was little better than a thief, then he was but a falcon who did Her Majesty's bidding.

"The tide is turning, Sam," said the admiral.

"Just now, my lord, it's true," said the captain, haggard and hollow-voiced. Ashes grizzled his dark beard.

"It'll be in full flood soon," said the admiral, "and we'll run with it. See, even the wind is with us now."

"They have new guns," said the captain.

"I've seen them," said the admiral. "Iron guns, six of them on the hillside. No, perhaps more than six. Make it ten or twelve. Will you wager with me whether they can put a shot between our masts?"

Despite his weariness our captain laughed, shaking his head. The good-hearted man was exhausted nearly to the point of a kind of bravado when he responded, "We shall either survive, my Lord Admiral, or we shall not."

The inconstant wind ceased altogether as the guns on the hill began to spew white smoke.

The reports of the guns reached us after a long moment, and the shots splashed near the *Golden Lion,* our sister warship following the pinnaces out to sea ahead of us. It was tempting to believe that the Spanish were giving us a farewell volley, a harmless salute. The morning sun in the sails was beautiful, the pennons of the *Golden Lion* flowing in the indolent wind. The open sea stretched far ahead of us—safety and freedom.

A leech crawling across a table makes a speedier progress than we could that morning. The ebbing tide carried us steadily but slowly, the lazy breeze drawing us into the range of the hillside battery. It was an anxious, bedeviling journey, our vessels making a stately parade under the eyes of our enemy.

Something howled through the air over our foremast. A cloud of smoke appeared over the hillside battery, and the heart-stopping thump of gunfire punished the air.

"They have our range, Admiral," said Captain Foxcroft.

Chapter

44

●

AHEAD OF US THE ENGLISH PINNACES were braving the passage past the fortification that defended the mouth of the harbor. The *Golden Lion* sailed right behind them, the water around her punished by the guns on the hillside, and the first shots from the fortress. Scribbles of smoke appeared everywhere along the shore closest to us, harquebus fire snapping across the water, smacking our hull.

Many of the harquebusiers, it seemed, had saved their powder for the passage of the admiral's vessel, harrying us as we brought up the rear of our escaping fleet. Angry wasps snapped through the air, gunshots humming through our rigging, barking splinters from our mainmast, answered by musket fire from our maindeck.

Ross Bagot reported to our captain that our gun deck cannons could not be raised to fire upward, into the high hillside battery. Jack Flagg and the tough-sinewed Chubbs deployed our quarterdeck gun, but it was plain even to my landsman's eye that the few maindeck guns we could bring into play were weak compared with the weapons dug in on both shores.

Soldiers who had hurried to take positions along the rocky shore now leveled firearms across their tripods, and took aim. When they vanished behind a sudden screen of smoke, vague figures reeling with the recoil, their shots spanked our canvas and rattled across our deck.

Ahead of us the *Golden Lion* was exchanging fire with the fortified battery at the harbor mouth. The beautiful warship shuddered, splinters rising and spinning into the sky as we watched. A cannon rose off her deck, flung high into the air and falling, from our distant vantage point, like a length of dark kindling back among her crew.

Captain Foxcroft proved a capable sailing man, teasing enough power from the wind to bring us past the blazing battery, our prow parting bits of broken timber from our sister ship. And we gained further speed as we loosed a broadside, our shots punching the stone face of the fortress. Dust rose from the puncture stars on the blue-stone walls as the Spanish gunners, the very men who the previous day had watched us sail by with no show of hostility, now rammed home charges and fired them with a frenzy.

But our ship's sails were full now, shaken out and swelling with the wind, a good breeze at our stern. We were too weary to raise a cheer, but the land began to fall away from us, the beach and the playful surf spreading wide on either side as we gained the open water, sea swells sending spray over our deck. The air was free of smoke and the stink of smoldering freight, and seabirds danced overhead.

The *Golden Lion* came-to, well out of the harbor, waiting for us in the easy waters ahead.

She had an ugly hole amidships and her gunports were smashed, but her rigging and masts looked, to my eye, largely intact. Our vessel swept close to her sister ship, every one of us straining forward to take in the sight of fellow mariners and fighting men, their faces, too, besmirched and etched with weariness.

A call was lifted from the *Golden Lion,* words I could not make out, followed by others, the message lost to me as a sea swell broke over our ship, a sudden bath of cold but welcome sea water.

Captain Foxcroft stepped before me to say, "Master surgeon, I'll have a crew row you across."

I must have gaped stupidly.

The captain had to peer into my eyes with a look of concern and expand his message. "Their master gunner has taken hurt, Tom," he said, speaking as though experienced in communicating with battle-stunned men. "A shot has smashed his leg, and—between us—their ship's surgeons are worse than helpless."

I nodded, as though I understood perfectly, but remained rooted to the spot.

Admiral Drake put his hand on my shoulder. "Their master gunner needs a surgeon, Tom, or he will die."

Chapter

45

●

VICE-ADMIRAL BOROUGH MET ME AS I
scrambled onto the ship.

I was half-drenched with sea water from my brief passage between the vessels, and my awkward climb up the side.
Standing beside the vice-admiral was the red-mustached
sergeant William and I had seen on that distant evening in
London—it seemed a lifetime ago—gazing down from this
very ship.

Vice-Admiral Borough offered me a bleak glance, and
in a voice leaden with pessimism said, "You should have a
look at what's happened." Hercules, carrying my surgeon's
satchel, followed me into the surgeon's cabin.

I was appalled at what I found there.

The drink-stunned surgeon of the *Golden Lion* was pros-
trate on the floor of his cabin, outfitted in a leather apron
and the round leather cap of a medical man, but unable to
do more than lift his head and mumble. His mate was little

better, propped in a corner in an enfeebled state. Red wine and vomit stained the floor around them.

Hercules attended to both men. "This one is drunk, sir," he reported. "And this one is also drunk."

My patient lay on the scarred pine-plank table, and he was in a terrible state.

A ligature had been applied to the leg above the master gunner's knee, as was proper, but the binding was too loose to pinch off the flow of blood. A first cut with a bone saw had been made, the skin parted and bleeding, and the injured man was struggling to sit up.

I worked quickly.

As I refastened the binding around his leg, tightening it, I had Hercules press a flask of aqua vitae to my patient's lips. The gunner was a strongly built man with a brown beard and powder burns, tiny black spots, seared into his features. His hands were clammy, but his pulse was strong.

"It was a culverin-shot," said the gunner, his lips trembling with pain, "one of the long Spanish cannon." The right leg was beyond saving, crushed so badly its mangled condition itself helped prevent bleeding. The gunner seized my arm imploringly, his eyes asking a question he could not put into words.

"We'll see you alive," I said, "and back in England."

"Are my mates unhurt?" the gunner was asking as I seized the handle of the mallet.

I brought the tool down just so, a firm tap, like a glazier freeing glass from a church window. Just that amount of force, and nothing more, and my patient fell back upon the table.

I selected one of my master's own bone saws, made by a blade smith in Whitechapel. I breathed a prayer to Our Lord that a wayward sinner might nonetheless be an implement of His will, words I had heard my master speak on occasions similar to this.

I lifted the saw.

And I could not use it.

Chapter
46

HERCULES STARED AT ME EXPECTANTLY.

But I was frozen, unable to put the teeth of this fine-steel saw into the flesh of the patient before me. I had never performed an amputation. I never would. All along I had been lucky in my medical challenges, able to meet the demands that had come my way.

But this operation was beyond me. My palms were wet, my vision blurred, my own poverty of talent and courage exposed.

I parted my lips, about to apologize to Hercules. You are apprentice to a novice, I wanted to say. It's your misfortune, Hercules, but that's the plain truth.

Be quick, Tom.

I heard my master's voice as clearly as the creak and groan of the ship's timbers around me.

"You don't have to worry about me," said Hercules, interrupting my inward thoughts.

I blinked.

"The sight of a cut-off leg," said Hercules, "won't bother me, sir, very much at all."

Tom—it's as easy as kiss-the-duchess.

It was easy for a man who heard mermaids speak, I wanted to tell him.

All too easy for a gentleman and scholar who should have known that guns sometimes explode.

To my surprise my hands knew what to do, acting without my will—as though my master guided them.

I cut off the injured leg above the knee, working speedily. Hercules attended me, as I instructed, lying over my patient's middle to keep his body from rolling with the easy motions of the ship. The ligature was well tied—there was little bleeding. The wet sap of living bone clotted the teeth of the saw but did not dull them, and the amputation was done before I could further doubt myself.

Vice-Admiral Borough visited my patient when I had made the gunner comfortable, dosed with tincture of opium. All evidence of the previous botched surgery, including the two surgeons, had been removed and mopped, the severed limb wrapped in linen and secured in my satchel.

The vice-admiral gave a nod as he examined the clean bandages I had applied, and the tidy order I had made of the cabin, mustard roots and dental-pinchers restored to their shelves.

"Well done, surgeon," he said.

I accompanied the vice-admiral to the quarterdeck, the *Elizabeth Bonaventure* not a bowshot away from us. She was indeed a handsome warship. Admiral Drake leaned against the quarterdeck rail, and even at this distance I could see him rising and falling on his tiptoes, looking my way and running his hand over the rail impatiently.

Drake lifted a hand, gesturing, *Hurry!*

Chapter
47

●

A GALE ROSE JUST AS I BID FAREWELL TO Vice-Admiral Borough.

The swells were deepening, the boat crawling up the face of one wave, and down the back of another. A storm was brewing.

The oarsmen gritted their teeth, rowing hard. As we approached, the faces of Jack Flagg and Anne peered anxiously down at me. The *Elizabeth Bonaventure* rose high and then plunged, nearly capsizing the boat and its crew of oarsmen.

Hercules carried the surgeon's satchel, with its additional burden. Even so encumbered, Hercules was able to clamber easily up the ladder of webbed cordage. But now the boat groaned against the hull of our ship, an abyss opening and shutting between our boat and the warship.

The boat's crew rowed frantically, escaping, leaving me positioned like a spider on the warship's hull. I dangled, clinging to the webbing with numb fingers. Seamen called out to me, and Anne's voice joined them, but I was strength-

less against the plunge of the ship, seas rising up and surrounding me, and nearly dragging me off the side.

I did not belong at sea, I reminded myself with a shud-
dering laugh, and this was further evidence.

I closed my eyes and hung on. And as I clung to the side
of the ship, I heard a voice.

Thomas.

In the fume and toss of the sea, wasn't there a shape, off
in the vapor spinning through the wind? A mermaid, as
surely as I was flesh and bone, a green, half-seen figure
spinning, gone.

Jack Flagg and Anne reached steadying arms, until I set my
feet on the deck of the *Elizabeth Bonaventure.*